TROPOS

BY JUG BROWN

To
Gary & Tamara
Love, A
Please Enjoy
A.
5/23

ACKNOWLEDGEMENTS

We wish to thank artist Ben Perkins (@Brattyben) for a superb book cover. Thank you Cortney Mayfield for helping us get this book published. More than anything, it can't be said enough that we couldn't have completed this book without the constant support of our generous life partners Karen Scholler and Darlene Mea, who gave us the space to dream and play. This story about a young man's journey is dedicated to the memory of our fathers.

"Dreams are toys."

Shakespeare, The Winter's Tale

PREFACE

"You're going to be the death of me yet Kato, I swear" said movie mogul Filipo "Phil" Giardia, shaking his slightly larger than normal head.

"Your Mother died too young, but I blame myself. It's my fault I didn't step up right away when you were 10 with no parents. I'll regret that to my dying day. That one's on me."

Kato Worsen stretched his long legs and yawned. "Don't be so hard on yourself, Uncle Phil. A small amount of blame should be mine. It's only fair."

Phil glared at his nephew, narrowed his beady eyes, and groaned.

"I made a promise to my sister on her deathbed that I would take care of you. I can picture her, as if it was yesterday. She looked up at me with the meanest expression, and threatened me with the evil eye – the Malocchio – and told me she would curse me all the way to hell and back, a Maledetto, if I didn't keep you safe. Damn her. Your mother was a witch."

Phil spit on the floor and crossed himself.

Phil stood up from his Louis XIV chair and adjusted his dark blue and purple velvet bathrobe. Kato Worsen was sitting, bored and slouched on the couch opposite him, working at his nails with an emery board. They were in Phil's gaudy Hollywood mansion, in a room appropriately called 'the hall of mirrors,' a long ornate room with 20 foot floor to ceiling windows on one side and mirrors and huge paintings on the other. Everything was gilded and over the top ornate, including the ceiling. The room, like the interior of his entire overwrought house, was inspired by the Palace of Versailles.

Kato Worsen looked at his uncle with an irritated 'what, this again?' expression. He was 28 years old, a 6'3" slim, movie star handsome hunk with perfect cheekbones and jawline, and thick black, longish hair artfully spiked to look mussed. He was wearing a light tee shirt under a cream colored linen jacket, and light gray slacks with Italian loafers. If stared at long enough, it might be assumed that he wore a tiny bit of makeup.

"So what kind of trouble are you in now?" demanded Phil.

Kato examined a nail he was working on, nodded with satisfaction, and looked up.

"I need to pay off a guy."

"How much? What for? Who do you owe?"

Kato raised his eyebrows and shrugged his shoulders.

"That would be $12,000. I made a few bets with the Donnely brothers. The bets didn't work out. The collector they sent after me is Dino Valenti."

"Dino Valenti!" Phil shook his head.

Kato went back to polishing another nail.

"Yeah. That's the guy."

"Dino Valenti! Do you know what he's gonna do to you if you don't pay?"

Kato shrugged again, not looking up from his nail work.

"Something painful, something most unpleasant, I'm sure."

"Damn straight! That guy doesn't mess around. If Shapiro has Dino on you. You're toast. He'll break you into pieces."

"Oh dear me." The boredom in his voice was thick as stucco.

"He'll dislocate your arm. He'll break your fingers."

Kato went back to his emery board, his boredom oozing.

"Ouch. Things are not looking good for yours truly."

"He'll mess up that handsome face of yours."

"Oh no. Not the face. Please anything but the face." Kato yawned.

"You're in big trouble." Phil wanted to slap Kato, wake him up.

"It really does kind of appear that way. Pity." Kato finished another nail, held it up and smiled at the results. Just then Phil doubled over with pain. He sat in his Louis XIV chair.

"Owwww." He held his stomach. "Owwww."

Kato kept to his manicure, and said blandly, "something wrong, uncle?"

"My stomach. Owww. Worrying about you gave me ulcers."

"You should see a doctor."

"I've seen doctors. They don't know anything." Phil hissed, clenching his teeth.

"That's too bad. You need a new doctor."

"Get the fuck out of here. I'll take care of Dino Valenti for you. Just get out. Leave! Owww."

Kato stood and put his emery board away.

"There's just one more thing. I need a place to lay low for a little while."

Phil looked at his nephew, with agony on his face. "What's wrong with your apartment in Marina Del Rey? It's beautiful."

"Sure, but I can't go there for a while."

"Why?"

"You remember Ashley LaVerne, the daughter of the 80's TV star, Heather Morrow?"

"No. Never heard of her."

"She was at one of your parties once. Doesn't matter. Anyway, she's suing me. She's trying to serve me papers. For assault and battery. I'm avoiding the process server."

"What have you got yourself into? Did you hit her?"

"No! Never! That's just her way to try to get some money out of me. No. I swear I never hit her. I never even touched her. I promise. That's the truth. I bought some, you know, product, and I kind of....you know....didn't pay her. She can't use the legal system to collect that type of debt, so she and her entourage are suing me for a phony assault and battery."

"Can you give her back the stuff?"

Kato winced, remembering his mad excessive cocaine use and his bloody noses.

"That's part of the problem. I don't want to give it back. I want to keep it."

Phil turned red with rage, frustration and physical pain.

"You're unbelievable! You can stay in the carriage house above the garage. Now get out! This is the last chance I'm giving you."

"Thanks uncle. You're the best."

Irv Gottlieb woke early. It was the hot penetrating sun shining a ribbon across his face that brought him out of his cocktail coma sleep. He was outside the pool house of his best friend and movie colleague, Filippo, 'Phil' Giardia, who, being the nicest guy in the movie making business, was always at Irv's disposal. Phil's house was Irv's safe haven and escape.

When he got his bearings, the first thought that came into his scheming mind was about the deferred maintenance that had plagued his own mansion for the past few years. He had not produced a show or a movie for that long. Yet, he stubbornly hung onto the house, despite the fact that he could have sold it to settle the alimony that diminished his bank account since the divorce became final.

His own house was a wreck. Besides the mess on the inside which was at the effect of his disorganized mental state, the slate roof had developed several profound cracks and the local earthquakes had made an area in the back half of his house begin to sink. Consequently a section of slate slid off, opening a gap that allowed water in. The water had begun rotting some of the cross beams and the ceiling was mostly ruined and smelled of fungus.

Despite these obvious alarms, Irv kept his cool – or was it his indifference? It was the Hollywood way: one endured, no matter what traumatic events came your way. One stayed the course, even faced with the dismal fact that Hollywood had forgotten him. It had moved on. Yet he maintained the illusion of success. Nothing was too big to ignore and tolerate as long as Irv was still recognized as being "in the game". He knew he could not keep up the appearance forever. It was inevitable that soon he would join the ranks of the has-beens. His last successful money making film was years ago. The fact that he was still hanging on by the skin of his teeth was solely due to the generosity of good old Phil Giardia, one of the revered kings of the Hollywood movie scene.

As Irv laid in his own alcoholic sweat. He remembered dancing the night before beside Phil's pool that was just outside the door. He recalled how he playfully pretended to drown so that the nubile bikini clad hostesses of the party would jump into the pool to "save" him. He remembered putting his arms around them and leaning against them to feel their presence. All to staunch his burning loneliness. His life had been without real connection for so many years, and Irv was not the kind of guy who went to prostitutes. He had tried the dating sites many times only to come away from them feeling more lonely than ever before, terminally lonely.

At that moment he remembered why he came to Phil's house. He needed money and Phil was the only person he could wheedle money from. He had a scheme fully hatched and this morning was the moment to put it into action. He got up and showered. He puked while the water pounded onto his black dyed comb-over. He practiced the script while he sobered up.

The story would be out today in Variety. He knew the reporter well and made sure it would include key statements that would feed his scheme. He toweled himself off and found a pair of swim trunks. He heard the maids setting up breakfast by the pool and waited until he heard Phil begin his morning coughing spell. The coughing was always accompanied by the smell of a Cuban cigar. It occurred seconds before Don Filippo made his entrance onto the pool deck.

"Morning Don Filippo," Irv said, trying to tweak his friend's vanity.

"Hey Irv. Glad you didn't drown last night, heh, heh." Phil puffed on his Cuban and watched the sun dancing on the pool water while the server poured his first espresso of the day.

"You should have joined us Phil."

"No thanks. Not my idea of fun."

"Your loss. It was dicey there for a minute, bro. But I recovered with a bit of help." Irv made a distinctly lurid hand gesture and Phil nodded back at him.

"I'll bet you did, lad." It was their way of referring to each other. Phil called Irv, "Lad". Irv called Phil, "Bro".

Irv approached the table and sat. He grabbed a few pieces of melon, put them onto his plate and tasted one using his soiled fingers.

"Ah. Another beautiful day in paradise," sighed Phil taking another sip of espresso.

Irv eyed the current edition of Variety folded on the table and rehearsed his spiel, awaiting the moment when Phil would pick it up. He thought about his ruined ceilings and the small pails in place to catch the rain and prevent further damage to the oak floors that were already covered with drop cloths. He expected the repairs would cost nearly half a million. He needed to keep his house. If he sold it, he would lose his status.

Irv's celebrity neighbors had never been inside his home. He built his reputation by attending their parties and being introduced as the executive producer that made Filippo Giardia's movies into great successes. Now his connection to his neighbors was reduced to a theatrical wave as he appeared with a flourish at his door to grab the morning newspaper when he saw them jogging past.

Irv was a schemer. It was how he made it in this business.

"Sleep well Phil?".

"Not too much sleep, Lad. Not last night. I don't feel right. I don't really sleep anymore." Phil leaned back and blew a big waft of smoke. The latest two of Irv's female lovelies came down to the pool in revealing bikinis and sat at the edge sipping glasses of fresh squeezed juice. They looked dazed and exhausted beneath their dewy starlet veneer as they idly kicked their toes to splash the water gently.

Irv watched as Phil picked up *Variety*. He waited eagerly to hear the response. He took a sip of tangerine juice and watched Phil turn the pages. He pretended to idly sip, but he knew exactly what page the news was on.

"Here it comes," Irv thought, "as soon as he turns this page." He cleared his throat and waited for his cue.

"What? This is ridiculous. What the fuck!"

"Hey Bro, what's the deal?" Irv said.

"They're saying I'm done, a has-been. This is bullshit." He put his cigar down.

"What, Phil?"

"How can they say my career is over? I own a movie studio."

"They said that?"

"It's plain as day, right here." Phil scowled.

"What're ya gonna do, bro? You can't just let them say that. You're in the middle of a great career here. How can they say that?" Irv feigned concern.

"I'll show them." Phil said angrily. Then he coughed weakly. "Girls, why don't you go inside now, or better yet, just go home, all of you. The party's over. We have some business to take care of here." The starlets rose with stereotyped obedience and headed into the house.

"Bro. I've got an idea. It's simple. Make a new movie." Irv thought about his sliding clay roof tiles and the cost of the mounting repairs.

Phil didn't pay attention.

"They say I've been out of touch for years. I can't let that stand. This is an insult. I'm not old? I'm not washed up. Am I?"

"No, of course not. Why don't we show them? I can help. We can make a fucking blockbuster. I've been reading a lot of scripts lately," he lied, "and there are some that are terrific, really relevant and amazing." He lied again.

"You think so, Irv? I don't know. It's a lot of pressure."

Suddenly Phil looked depressed, pale-faced and old. Was Phil through? If so, it would be hard to blame him for wanting to avoid the serious exhaustion of making a movie. Phil knew better than anyone about the pressure, the details, the daily list of people to contact, the worries, the actors and their contracts and the diddling requests that never ended. The entire litany of personalities and their quirky disorders was why he might want to retreat from the industry. The incidents and idiosyncrasies and demands flashed through his memory and he reviled once again. This was Irv's cue.

"I have an idea Bro. I've got some choice scriptwriters on my list. I've read a number of pieces and I can be ready to go very soon. Why don't you leave it to me? We've got history, you and me. We know how to make it happen. Let's do it!" Irv added with a tone of confidence.

"Lad, I'm not so sure we..."

"Bro, I got this. No worries. It's in the bag. I can get these guys on the payroll and they'll be under my whip hand. I'll kick their asses into high gear. C'mon, what's the worst thing that can happen?"

"I don't know." Phil looked off at his neighbor's turreted estate, visible above his twenty foot laurel hedge. "I just don't know, Lad." Phil took a deep draught from his glass and shook his head.

"Tell me, Lad. Am I a has-been?"

"Of course not. You've been on hiatus. An extended one, yes, but you're right there, ready to spring into action."

"I don't know if I want to spring into action anymore. I'm tired of the hassles." Phil shook his head.

"You can't let them say this about you, Bro. It's just not right. You've been the king of the blockbusters. You rode the horse to the top of the hill. You killed the giant, you found the holy grail. You've made careers for many actors. You've got favors you can call in. And here's the good part, Bro. All you have to do is sign the checks. I'll do all the dirty work. All the heavy lifting. And I'm ready to go!" Irv delivered his best right hook into the belly of the beast. His excitement level lifted at the right moment. His need for money carried his monologue. It was a gifted speech.

"You can do this for me, Lad?" Phil Shrugged.

Of course money was not an issue. Phil had a couple hundred million always ready. Irv knew this and was instead aiming for the majesty of Phil's ego that once stood near the vaunted heights of fame on the hallowed ground of the stars, like a rearing steed.

"Okay Lad. We're on! Let's do this." Phil began to walk around the table. He picked up a croissant and nibbled as he thought it over, pacing back and forth in front of the table.

After a few minutes, Phil said.

"However, there is one thing, Lad. I'll finance the project, but you've gotta put Kato on the payroll. I've gotta get him out of my hair. I'm giving him one more chance. He's driving me crazy."

Irv groaned and shook his head. He thought, "Not Kato, please. I haven't seen him for a while. I hope he hasn't gotten worse."

Phil responded to Irv's groan, "Yeah, I know. I can't blame you Irv, but I made a promise to my sister."

Irv was irritated. Kato was a problem that had to be avoided.

"Phil, I'm sorry, but I'm tired of hearing for the thousandth time about your promise to your sister. When Kato was a little kid, right after she died, I was there for him and for you. Hell, he even lived at my house half the time. You and I both took him to sports and stuff. Early on, I devoted myself to that boy. He was sweet. I loved him."

"He was a great kid. The best. He was generous. He was funny. And then he hit puberty," said Phil, reciting the facts they both knew so well.

"Right," said Irv. "He hit puberty and all of a sudden, this sweet kid we knew turned into a monster in front of our eyes. He wasn't sweet anymore. He wouldn't listen. He was angry. It went downhill fast. I tried to set boundaries, he violated them. He stole from me, he stole from you, he hung around with the wrong crowd. When he took my Ferrari for a joy ride the night of his high school graduation party and crashed it, I was done. I had enough. I told him never to come back to my house. And there is no possibility of him being on any movie project I am working on. None at all."

"I know Irv. You kicked him out of your life. You did the right thing, for you. But, I just can't do that to him. I made a promise."

Irv groaned.

"So okay, you want me to take Kato back and give him a place in my movie. Has he changed at all?"

Phil shook his head, sorrowful and disgusted.

"I can't say he's changed. But I do know he's around the house all the fucking time. He's a pain in the ass. He thinks he's hot shit. He comes and goes as he pleases, and I got to be here and support his fucking behavior." Phil was exasperated. His blood filled face looked like a tight balloon.

"Kick him out already. It's tough love for god's sake. He needs it."

"I made a promise."

Irv groaned.

"Irv, tell you what. I'm gonna greenlight the movie, even without reading the script, but you've gotta put Kato up somewhere, and do it soon. I don't care what you do with him. Just get him out of my hair, Lad." Phil continued to pace, and as he did sweat shined on his wet red cheeks.

Irv gave in. There was no use arguing. Phil was on the hook. He knew he had to close fast. With a check in hand he could engage the writers and start the contractors on the house. Maybe he could keep Kato on a short leash.

"All I need is a check to get started, Phil."

"Okay, Okay. Let's do this. Martha! Martha!" A small hispanic woman magically appeared on the patio.

"Martha bring me the checkbook, please. The big business one on the back shelf."

"Yes Mr. Phil." She smiled pleasantly, turned and left.

"I can make the calls today. We can't let this news report stand. I'll let them know we've started production on a new film of great scope and magnitude. We'll get your reputation back, Phil. You'll be on top again before the end of the day."

Irv wondered how quickly he could get a contractor to start the roof of his mansion. The rainy season would be starting in just a few months.

Martha appeared and handed Phil the checkbook.

"How much do you need, Lad, three million?"

"That'll be enough to get the ball rolling. We'll need more later on."

Irv knew he could get some screenwriters on board for cheap, and this check would cover the foundation repairs and the roof rebuild without even a second thought.

"Here you go Lad. Let's make it happen." Phil poured a glass of vodka for Irv, and an orange juice for himself, and they toasted to making another movie together.

PART 1
SHOWDOWN AT THE LOVE DOG RANCH

Chapter 1

Late August, Friday afternoon, six weeks later

The first of the three screenwriters to arrive at Love Dog Ranch in Eastern Oregon for the intensive, no-distractions, marathon screenwriting retreat was Brent Gardner.

He brought his tricked out red and white 4x4 Dodge Diesel pickup, complete with a row of lights on the roof and a heavy duty trailer hitch, to a stop in a cloud of dust in front of the log cabin lodge, destined to be his home for the next month.

He slowly unpacked his overweight, 52 year old, 6'2" body out of the truck. Frowning at the dust on his nice truck, he took out a bandana and wiped clean the logo on the door, "Evictus Ranch, Settlers Pass, Montana." He adjusted his immaculate cream colored cowboy hat, checkered western shirt and stood in the empty stillness of the hot afternoon. He took in the surroundings. The cook's car was already there, a black, late model Mercedes SUV. *Pretty nice car for a cook,* thought Brent.

Brent fashioned himself a rancher. Underneath his hat he had a large block of a head, with a full head of light brown hair that was trimmed into an old fashioned, no nonsense 1950's flat top. He wasn't prone to smiling, and when he did, it was usually to enjoy the discomfort or embarrassment of others. He looked just like a lifelong conservative cattleman.

But the cattleman part and the crew-cut Republican looks were recent additions. Until 5 years ago, Brent Gardner had been a fashionable, well dressed Los Angeles realtor specializing in rent collection for large apartment complexes. "Maximize your rent with Brent!" was the slogan that made him a multi millionaire and the favorite of absentee apartment building owners hailing from Dubai to Dallas. He was known to be ruthless, incapable of compassion, and perfectly at home in courtrooms, boardrooms and ad agencies. He knew all the wealthy players in LA and Hollywood real estate.

He grew up a Southern California boy from Torrance, the only child of two CPA's. They were into money making, and he followed their footsteps. He sold his soul to greed first as a realtor and then a rent collection specialist. After many very successful years, he sold his rent collecting empire and left LA to pursue his dream of becoming a big sky rancher in Montana.

When he retired to his ranch five years ago at age 47, he was a fish out of water on the wide open prairie. He could evict poor LA families out of their apartments as easily as a sumo wrestler could toss a 5 year old child, but he couldn't rope a calf, and he couldn't ride a horse. He didn't have any ranching skills, but he did have the deed to a 4,700 acre spread, a rancher's truck, a rancher's haircut, and most importantly he had the hat.

He quickly learned to enjoy cattle branding and castration and yukking it up with his hired hands, which in the summer included a few paid interns, who were the sons and daughters of his old wealthy Los Angeles real estate clients. He looked the part of a rancher. He fashioned himself as "one lonely man upholding the sacred ideals and traditions of the white man's destiny in the west". He had been married and divorced three times before age 35, before he realized that marriage was never going to improve his bottom line.

Brent was a history buff of the old west. The one that interested him most recently was a true story. He researched it, and then sold this story to Irv Gottlieb, movie producer and former real estate client. The story centered on the misadventures of a 1968 hippie commune in rural Montana that occupied 80 acres of ranch land. The hippies' land was surrounded in every direction by 100,000 acres owned by a hostile ranch family. The story of the many conflicts intrigued him. He wrote it up into a synopsis on a whim. He was surprised to find out that it was good enough to convince Irv. He called the movie "When the Love Left."

Accordingly, Irv arranged a month-long intensive screenwriter retreat to hammer out a screenplay. When Brent sold the story rights, he insisted that he be included in the screenwriting team. Even though he had never written a screenplay, Irv relented and told Brent he could be part of the team. Irv had a team in mind: A journeyman well-experienced screenwriter and an up and coming whiz bang idea guy.

Brent stood in front of the two story, steep roofed, luxury ski lodge-looking building. A sign above the front door read "Antelope Room." A full porch went all around the front and side of the house with heavy rustic log chairs and a porch swing.

There was an identical, much smaller log cabin across the half acre parking lot. A hundred yards away was a 60 foot long empty dog kennel, with chain link runs, that were long ago overgrown with weeds. There was an unused windmill swaying in the breeze near the kennels next to a large stock tank.

Brent looked away from the buildings. There were only a few trees close by, a handful of large cottonwoods over by the kennels. There were a couple of chairs under them. The rest of what he saw was rolling sagebrush country, and distant blue shadowed hills. It was lonely, empty land, 40 miles from the back side of Oregon nowhere. It was land that was too hot in the summer, and too cold at night. When Brent looked up, the late afternoon sky was a perfectly clear, cloudless blue dome. It was a land of contrasts. This was empty country. The simple majestic features of the land, the sky, the sun, the distant barren hills, the monotonous sagebrush and the constant wind had a harsh magnificence to it.

It was land whose beauty was easily capable in one moment of inspiring awe, reverence, and a close personal connection to God, while in the next moment, this same place could turn on you, and inspire panic to your core. It could make a person feel puny and afraid, lonely, insignificant, and vulnerable. This country could force one to believe that the only solution to this terrifying alone-ness was to slit one's wrists just to escape. It was that type of place; profound in its depth of both beauty and abject solitary horror.

Brent took it all in. He felt and understood the majesty of its forlorn, hopeless loneliness. He took a deep breath and pushed his cowboy hat back on his head. *It's perfect, I love it out here,* he said to himself.

Chapter 2

Brent wheeled his suitcase up the porch stairs and paused briefly before pushing the massive double doors open without knocking or announcing himself. This was his idea of what a real rancher would do. He stopped and liked what he saw.

The Antelope Room was a massive 75 foot square room, all log walls and wood trim, with a 30 foot ceiling. Opposite him was an enormous river rock fireplace going all the way up to the peak of the steep roof. To the left of the fireplace was a grand staircase leading up to the second story balcony.

But to Brent what most impressed him were the mounted heads of game animals covering three of the walls. One entire wall had antelopes and deer, but the other walls held elk, black bear, mountain lion, lynx, wolverine, and an African lion. Brent thought they must have come from the same taxidermist, because the eyes were the same, highly reflective green and gold flecked, resembling animal eyes caught at night in a car's headlights. They were unnatural. In the corner, next to the fireplace was the head of a huge grizzly bear, and underneath it was an old rifle that Brent couldn't see too clearly.

The furniture in the Antelope Room was spare. Two big overstuffed leather sofas and two arm chairs surrounded a large low table made from slabs of old growth wood polished to a sheen. The floor was gray flagstone. A few expensive oriental rugs covered the area around the coffee table, but the rest of the floor was bare. An enormous chandelier made from dozens of antlers hung from the ceiling above the coffee table.

Standing at the door to his right was a gleaming commercial quality kitchen, open to the room, and in front of the kitchen was a dining table designed to seat 10 people easily, made of the same slabs of old growth wood. The chairs were heavy wrought iron with thin cushions. Taken as a whole, the place looked less like a hunting lodge, and more like the opulent great room of a medieval castle. The walls nearest the kitchen area had no animal trophies, but were instead covered with museum quality paintings of dogs. There were new paintings, old paintings, abstract paintings, and one section of the wall closest to the kitchen had photographs and prize ribbons.

A man popped his head out the pantry in the kitchen. He was tall, fit and twenty something, stylishly dressed, with longish black hair that was well cut and long on the sides with careful moussed and cowlicked spikes randomly spaced on top and back. He had a handsome beak of a nose, perfect cheekbones and a movie star jawline. His eyebrows were dark black over intense brown eyes. He was dressed in a flowered Hawaiian shirt and black jeans. He was wearing a waiter's apron.

To Brent, he didn't look like a cook. He had the handsome good looks of a male model. For another thing, his eyes were darting around the room. They were hard eyes. He was no meek cook. He looked like a predator.

"You must be Brent," he said. "I'm Kato."

"You're the cook."

"That's right. I'm here to make your stay here productive and smooth." They shook hands.

"This is a big spread. Are there any ranch hands living here taking care of the place?" asked Brent.

"Nope. It will just be the four of us. We will be alone. I have a fully stocked freezer. We are self-sufficient for the entire month."

"So where do I put my things?"

"There are three bedrooms. One bedroom upstairs is the master bedroom, and there are two small bedrooms downstairs. I was told that it was first come, first serve."

Brent only took a second to answer.

"I'll take the master bedroom."

Kato shrugged.

"I'm preparing dinner. We'll eat as soon as the others get here. They're about a half hour out. We're going to have a different cuisine every night this first week. You're going to love it. Tonight is Thai. I'm making my special eggplant Basil stir fry, a Thai salad with thinly sliced marinated beef, ice tea and coconut ice cream for dessert.

"Sounds delicious. I think I'll get settled."

Kato nodded and went back to preparing the food. But first, he turned on some music -- loud. To Brent it sounded like gangster rap, but the rapper had an irritating, artificially altered robot voice.

Brent walked across the room to the staircase, and paused at the enormous snarling grizzly bear head. When he got near, the green and gold flecked eyes came alive in the chandelier light. It was a bit unnerving. He looked at the rifle in a custom designed display case. It was unlocked. Brent took down the rifle, and whistled to himself. It was a Winchester model 1866 in perfect condition, with gleaming brass. He reverently worked the lever. It was smooth. He held up the rifle to the sunlight and looked down the barrel. It was clean and well oiled. *The gun that won the west. This one killed this huge grizzly bear.* Brent carefully put back the gun, noticing the box of bullets on the shelf inside the case.

He went up the grand staircase. The balcony spanned one side of the great room below. There were two doors. He opened the first. The master bedroom was a large light-filled room with a panoramic view of the distant mountain and a king sized bed. He put his bag down and walked through the rest of the suite. There was a large bathroom, with a shower, a tub, and a sauna. There was a walk-in closet. He tried a door opposite the bed and found himself in a sitting room, complete with a desk under another large window, and a futon couch.

"*I like it,*" Brent said to himself. "*This room will be my office.*

Chapter 3

As Brent was unpacking, the next screenwriter arrived in his own cloud of Oregon dust, and parked his unimpressive 20 year old Subaru Forester next to Brent's truck. Walter Journey (Walt to his friends) slowly emerged from the car and got his two bags from the back. He stood in the afternoon heat and slowly took a look around. Everything he did was slow these days. It was something he had taught himself after a life of bitter experiences. He was 55 years old, a bit overweight, with a nonathletic body, a squarish head and a receding hairline. He was kind looking, but his jowls gave him a sad, hound dog appearance.

Walt Journey possessed one remarkable natural feature: he had a radio perfect, deep baritone voice. It was a pleasing voice that had an abundance of volume and richness. It was a singer's voice; he had sung for 20 years in the Bakersfield community choir. His remarkable voice had often been described as a cross between the soothing voices of Walter Cronkite and Charles Kuralt, and in fact, Walt resembled Charles Kuralt a bit.

Walt was a former experienced LA screenwriter, who infamously burned out 25 years ago, and was now leading a quiet life as a community college English teacher in Bakersfield, California. Six weeks ago, Walt had never expected in a million years to be called up out of the blue to write another screenplay. When Irv called him and pitched the month-long isolated retreat of a three man team to write a screenplay for 'When the Love Left', he first talked the idea over with his wife (his third). After carefully weighing the pros and cons, they decided he should take the job for the extra income it would provide, and for the possibility of getting other screenwriting gigs in the future.

Now he was here in the Oregon sagebrush desert. He picked up his bags and walked to the front door, noticing the sign: Love Dog Ranch, Antelope Room. He politely knocked. There was no answer. He heard loud rap music from inside. He politely knocked again. This time, the door flew open and an impatient, intense, stylishly dressed young man took one look at Walt before walking away.

"I'm cooking. You didn't need to knock. This is your home."

"Good to know," said Walt in his radio perfect baritone, "I'm Walter, but call me Walt."

Kato was back in the kitchen, chopping food rapidly.

"I know who you are. I'm Kato. Brent is already here. He's upstairs. He took the upstairs bedroom. You can have one of the two downstairs bedrooms." He pointed with his cleaver towards two doors on the left wall and went back to his chopping.

There was something about Kato, and his entire demeanor, that caused Walt to pause for a moment. He watched Kato's quick movements, his darting eyes, his stylish clothes, money to burn, and his carefully tended model good looks. Then he realized what he saw in Kato: If Walt were back in Hollywood during his bad old days, and if Walt was in a party of strangers and if Walt wanted to score some dope, this guy would be the sure bet to get connected.

Kato looked like someone who had recently been strung out. He was a bit too thin, a bit too quick. Walt knew Hollywood flash when he saw it. Kato was another of the countless hangers on around the show business world, one of the many who never made it, for any number of reasons, including lack of talent, addiction issues, anger issues, lack of connections, or poor impulse control. *Yeah,* thought Walt. *I know him, a spoiled Hollywood brat. What is he doing here, as a cook? How is that going to work? He doesn't look like a gofer.*

Walt went to the two doors side by side, with a full bathroom next to them. He opened the first door. The rap music in the background was now mixing with the sound of Kato making a sizzling stir fry. The first door opened to a kids room. It was outer space and animal themed. It had a bunk bed, Batman sheets and spaceship blankets, a small window, and a small desk. There were stars and spaceships and animals painted on the light blue walls. Walt closed the door, and opened the door to the other bedroom. He was pleased. This second bedroom was spacious, with a queen sized bed, a large window, a large desk, and oil paintings of horses and dogs on the walls. *I'll take this one.*

Walt didn't have time to unpack before the rap music stopped and Kato called out loudly:

"Dinner is ready. Brent, Walt, hurry up, come on out! Julien is here."

Walt left his bags on the bed and went out.

Chapter 4

The third screenwriter arrived just after Walt. Julien, 'JJ' Pinkus drove up in a restored 1985 Mazda RX-7. He was in his early 20's, 5'8'' and 130 pounds with short dark hair. He was wearing dark jeans and a baggy Green Day tee shirt. He was apprehensive at being here. He was not comfortable around people at all. He wasn't interested in them. Diagnosed with Aspergers early on, he didn't work well with others. Though he worked on his behavior, he was naturally impatient. He was easily angered and wasn't well liked or understood.

In the vicious world of insider movie business twitter gossip, the settled opinion was he was an "Irritating, antisocial techno-dweeb." Early in life he discovered that he loved creative work. Before being called up unexpectedly for this project, he was involved in a number of original projects in various stages of readiness to pitch to studios.

JJ's first success came at age 15, when, working alone in his bedroom, he created and promoted a 30 second Instagram video of supposedly tame animals biting, kicking, scratching or injuring humans in hilarious ways. It went viral and got 90 million views in two weeks making JJ famous for a brief moment. He became interested in making films, and this led him to USC film school. He lasted only a year, but that was all he needed of formal education. After 12 months he was way ahead of his classmates.

He was known as an up and coming wunderkind in the film business, but had yet to work on a big production. He took this screenwriting gig in the desert for the sole purpose of building his resume, and more importantly to get access to people who could take a look at his current projects. He wanted to make big projects. He knew this was going to be difficult because he didn't like to be around people. His natural impatience led him to get bored easily. It was excruciating to sit through meetings and do a lot of detailed team work with others. He worked best alone.

JJ was on the porch when he heard Kato shouting that dinner was ready. He entered the lodge without knocking. As soon as he got through the door, Kato nodded at him. Kato turned off the music. JJ set his bags down by the door. Kato pointed at the big 10 person table and JJ took a seat on the side. Brent and then Walt walked over. The men all shook hands and said their names quickly. Kato brought out food.

"Sit, sit!" he ordered. "Eat now, talk later."

Brent gravitated towards the head of the table and sat down. JJ was to his right, and Walt took the place to his left. Kato set out the food.

They started eating. "This is amazing," said Walt in his radio perfect voice. The others murmured their assent. Kato smiled proudly.

"We will have cuisine from a different country every night this week." He sat next to Walt.

"If this is how we're going to eat, I'm already impressed with this gathering," said Brent.

"A good start," said Walt between mouthfuls.

JJ didn't say anything. Small talk was difficult for him.

They finished the main course and Kato brought out coconut ice cream for dessert. "Coffee anyone?"

"Sure," boomed Brent. "

"I'll stick with this Thai ice tea," said Walt.

"Say, Kato, how about a little bump in this coffee. Any liquor here?" said Brent.

"Absolutely," said Kato. He got up and opened a cabinet next to the pantry filled with bottles.

"We are fully stocked. Top shelf stuff too. Help yourself."

Brent took his coffee and poured in a slug of Wild Turkey bourbon, "Can I get something for you fellas?"

"Nothing for me," said Walt.

"I'm good," said JJ, shaking his head.

Brent sat down at the table as Kato cleared the dishes. He took a big drink of his spiked coffee and decided to take charge of things. He said, "Why don't we introduce ourselves? I'll go first."

Chapter 5

"Well," drawled Brent, leaning forward "My name is Brent Gardner. I have a big spread up in Montana. We run cattle, a few hundred sheep. It's a good life, even if it's hard and not for everyone. I came up with the idea for this movie, "When the Love Left". It's my idea, and it's based on a true story that happened up in those parts in 1968, and I hope we tell it like it happened. I could have written the screenplay myself, but Mr. Gottlieb insisted that I use you all. And that's about all I have to say."

Brent made no mention of his LA surfer boy roots, his affluent parents, skiing in Tahoe during the winters. He didn't mention the Los Angeles real estate and rent collecting business he sold when he bought his ranch a few years ago. He was trying to pass himself off as just a plain talking cowboy.

"What about you?" he said somewhat aggressively, looking at Walt.

Walt blinked, and took a few seconds to answer. Brent was pushy.

"My name's Walt Journey. I wrote and edited screenplays back in the 90's and early 2000's. I worked with several big names, including Lucas films once, Spielberg once, and I have credits on a few other big films. I left Hollywood 25 years ago. I'm a college professor now. It was a good surprise to be called. I'm glad to be working once again. I look forward to getting to know both of you."

Walt made no mention of his disgraceful flame out in the business, his alcoholism, his 25 years of careful sobriety, or all the bridges he burned as he ruined his life. He looked at JJ.

"Ok," said JJ in a soft voice, without looking directly at anyone.

"My name is Julien Pinkus, but please call me JJ. I live in LA. I have several projects in the works to pitch to studios. One is a time travel story in which the traveler must go back and meet her grandparents, but she gets kidnapped in the past by their enemies. She gets back to the present, but must then go into the future to fix things. Another is an animation project based on a Japanese folk hero. I have a courtroom drama in the works, and a Jason Bourne type action adventure spy thriller too. Hopefully I will be pitching at least one of these ideas soon to Irv Gottlieb."

JJ made no mention that he knew that nobody really liked working with him, or that he had been bluntly informed on numerous occasions that he was too aloof, touchy and inflexible. JJ looked at Kato.

Kato leaned his long arms on the table in front of his highball glass, "My name is Kato Worsen. I've worked on this and that, some movies, some modeling, understudy for a reality show, some commercials. I haven't landed an acting part yet, but I'm hopeful, just like everybody." He smiled. He crossed his fingers and held them up.

He made no mention that he was the nephew to the studio boss Filipo "Phil" Giardia, who got him this gig. Nor did he mention that in his troubled attempts at employment, he had failed in every Hollywood gig he had ever attempted, for a long list of reasons. He also failed to mention that he was out here in the desert to avoid being served papers in a civil case of assault and battery brought by a woman who foolishly fronted Kato a half ounce of pure coke. When she tried to collect, Kato laughed and refused to pay. She was furious. She couldn't sue for the debt, so she made up the assault and battery civil case.

JJ got up from the table. "I think I need to get settled in my room, but first I want you to meet my support animals."

He went to the front door and came back with his bags and a small soft animal crate. He put the crate on the floor, reached in and brought out two identical tawny and dark brown ferrets, each with a white blaze on the forehead. He put the ferrets on his shoulders and they immediately disappeared into his tee shirt, poking their heads out of the sleeves.

"I would like all of you to meet 'The Flying Ferretinis', my special pets and emotional-companion-support animals. This is Klaus," said JJ, taking one ferret out of his sleeve and putting it on the table, "and this is Villy. The Ferretinis are fully housebroken."

The ferrets started scampering around the table, making little noises, sniffing and checking out everything. They seemed to explore as a team. First they checked out Brent from a few feet away. He put out a hand to greet them, but they kept away. Then they came up to Walt briefly, sniffed the air and moved away.

When the ferrets came to Kato, one of them immediately jumped on Kato's arm and climbed into his hands. Kato made a smooching sound. Kato took a stick of carrot and put it into his mouth. He held the ferret up to his face and the animal started munching the carrot out of Kato's mouth. When the ferret pulled the carrot out of Kato's mouth, Kato gently put the ferret back on the table and it scampered across the table to JJ.

"I love those ferrets!" said Kato. "Thank you for bringing them."

"That one is Villy," said JJ. "He likes you Kato. He only likes a few people. Klaus is not friendly. He only lets me hold him. Well, it's time to see my room." He picked up the ferrets and put them back in their carrier.

"It was first come, first served for rooms. You have the room on the left downstairs," said Kato with a sneaky smile that Brent picked up on. Brent chuckled and sat back in his chair.

Chapter 6

JJ took one look at the kid's room with the bunk beds, the Batman sheets and the other little kid effects, and turned to the group who were sitting across the big hall at the big dining table.

"Is this some kind of a joke?" he demanded.

Brent smiled some more.

"No, not at all," said Kato, who was also clearly enjoying this.

"Irv told me the rooms were first come, first served. You got here last is all."

"That's fair," said Brent, nodding his head.

"What? Are you telling me those are the only rooms here? No way."

JJ looked in the room next door with Walt's stuff on the bed. "What about upstairs? It's huge."

JJ didn't wait for an answer. He ran up the staircase. At the top he started opening doors. A few seconds later, he emerged and stood at the balcony railing overlooking the great room.

"There are two big rooms up here. Why can't I have the second one?"

Brent shook his head, "That second room is part of the master suite, I got here first, so I claimed the entire upstairs suite. That second room is mine too, it's connected to the rest of the master bedroom. Right Kato?"

Kato nodded, smiling. "He's right JJ.".

JJ ran down the stairs. He stood in front of the table, his face flushed with rage,

"You have to give me that extra room. We should all have equal rooms."

Walt was looking down, not looking at anyone.

Brent shook his big head solemnly, "No, son, that's not the way it works. Up in Montana where I hail from, a man's property rights come first, they're sacred, and a man has to defend what is rightfully his. He is all alone. That's the law of the west. Once you start giving in, where does it stop? It doesn't. So I say hell no. You have a room, so take it." He sat back with a proud, smug look on his big blocky face. Kato was leaning against the sink. He pulled out a vape pen, and took in a large lungful. He looked pleased.

JJ pointed across the parking lot at the guest house, "Why can't I stay there? There has to be plenty of room in there."

"No. Not only was I the first one here, but Irv Gottlieb said I would get the guest house, so the screenwriters would have unfettered access to each other non-stop through the month. If I let you live there, it would ruin the Feng Shui I carefully created in my personal space, and it would keep the three of you from having the close quarters you need for your work experience. No JJ. You can't stay in my guest house." Kato was clear and exacting in his manner.

JJ 's face turned angry red, it became pointed like a dried fruit. "Why are you being such assholes?"

"Now wait a cotton picking minute, kid," said Brent, with a sudden snarl, "I don't care who you think you are, there's no need for that kind of cussing. That's just plain unnecessary. Don't be a crybaby." Brent looked to Kato, who mimicked Brent's solemn demeanor. JJ stood there and fumed.

Finally Walt looked up. He took a deep breath and exhaled, "Enough. Enough already," he said rather loudly in his radio perfect baritone. He looked at each of them in turn, finally ending with JJ.

"JJ, you can take the room I'm in. It's all yours. I'll take the small room. For crying out loud, I'm here to work, to creatively prosper with the two of you. I'm not here for the room I sleep in. It's a bed, right? That's all it is. We're professionals."

JJ didn't move.

"Well. Will you switch rooms with me, and finish this nonsense?" asked Walt.

"Hmmm. Ok," JJ agreed, but was not satisfied. He added, "You shouldn't have to stay in that little room either. It's an insult." JJ wanted to prolong the dispute. His sharp face bobbed like an agitated chicken.

Walt shook his head, "Forget it. Just forget it, please." Just then Kato's laptop beeped. He looked at the screen.

"Oh it's time for Irv Gottlieb's nightly call. He's going to check in at 6pm every night."

JJ didn't move.

"Sit down JJ. We have to take this call," said Kato.

"Don't ruin the call JJ," added Brent. "Sit down. Put on your game face. Be a professional."

JJ sat and scowled. Kato opened the laptop and instantly the four of them appeared on the screen, next to Irv Gottlieb's smiling face. He was by the pool. A pretty girl was sitting next to him wearing a bikini, with a bored expression. She was reading a fashion magazine.

"Fellas! Good to see you all made it," said Irv. "What a place I got for you, didn't I? You're going to love it up there. Fresh air, not like here in California. We have smog today so thick you could cut it into steaks. It's sick. And there you are, in the wilderness. Clean air. Clean living. No distractions. No disputes or bothers. I expect great things."

Brent took charge. He leaned forward, "Good to see you again Irv."

"Likewise Brent. How are the accommodations?"

Brent nodded his head, "They're fine, fine, fine." He looked directly at JJ, with a look of dare, "They're fine. Right JJ, right Walt?"

JJ scowled.

Walt played peacemaker. "The rooms are fine. Beautiful place here. Inspiring. Kato cooked us all a wonderful meal. I've never had better Thai food."

"I'll say," said Brent. Kato smiled at the compliment. JJ sat glumly and nodded his head slightly.

"That's the spirit fellas. Well you must be tired. We'll talk tomorrow, and you can tell me about your ideas for the screenplay. I need something real good, real original, and real fast most of all. I'm talking about award quality. I mean it. This story can do it. Aim for the stars. I can smell the success all the way down here. Oh wait, that's the smog." He laughed a hearty fake sounding laugh, looking at the woman, who cringed and went back to her magazine. Irv cut the connection.

"Jesus Christ," said JJ, still mad as hell.

"Don't take the Lord's name in vain around me, Julien." Brent hadn't been in a church for decades, and then only for a wedding that lasted two bitter years.

"My name is JJ. That's what I said."

Brent smiled his cruel smile; he was getting under JJ's skin again.

"I can't believe I'm doing this for a month for only $6,000!" said JJ.

Everyone became silent. Nobody moved. JJ looked around.

"Well. That's what we're all getting right? $6,000?"

Nobody said a word. Nobody moved. A long moment passed.

"You mean you're not getting $6,000?" JJ looked at each of them in turn.

Brent's mean smile returned. "I signed on for $15,000. This is my story. Remember what I said about the law of the west and a man's worth?"

"Shit," said JJ. He turned to Walt, "What about you? Are you getting $15,000 too?"

Walt paused, gathering his thoughts, and then in his most soothing voice said: "No JJ, I'm not getting $15,000."

"You're not? Unbelievable. How much then?"

"I'm getting scale screenwriter wages, $25,000."

Brent sat up. Now he was mad also.

"You're getting $25,000, and I'm only getting $15,000?"

Walt shook his head. He had a sympathetic look on his jowly hound dog face, "I have the experience. I'm entitled to scale."

"And I'm not?" Boomed Brent.

"Yeah. I agree with Brent. What about me?" said a very offended JJ, "Why don't I get scale?"

The three of them sat there. Kato leaned back against the sink. He had a big snide smile as he took a hit off his vape pen.

Brent looked at Kato, "What are you smiling at?"

Kato grinned.

"How much are you getting," demanded Brent.

Kato let out a cloud of vaped nicotine. "$35,000."

"What!!" exclaimed the screenwriters in unison. They all looked at Kato.

"A cook gets almost three times more than me?"

"Six times as much as me," said JJ.

Kato looked at all of them. "Phil Giardia is my uncle. I'm the most valuable person here. I have excellent experience and impeccable connections. I'm equal to any of you."

Brent pushed his heavy wrought iron chair back. It made a terrible loud noise on the flagstone floor, "This is wrong."

"Yes. This is nuts," said JJ, "This is unacceptable. I say we bring it up and settle this once and for all with Irv Gottlieb tomorrow night when he checks in. What do you say?"

"Agreed," said Brent.

"Agreed," said Walt.

Chapter 7

Next day, Saturday morning

The hostility between Brent and JJ heated up right away the next morning. Kato was in the kitchen early, this time sitting at the table with his laptop and a legal pad for taking notes. He didn't offer to make breakfast for anybody. He didn't even make coffee. The men scrounged in the pantry, and Brent made a pot of what he called 'cowboy coffee' by dumping some grounds in a saucepan and boiling it.

"This is what we drink out on the range." He poured Walt a cup, who tasted it and cringed.

JJ declined. He opened his laptop. The ferrets spent some time crawling over him, in and out of his sleeves and the neck of his tee shirt. Then they jumped off the table and went exploring around the great hall. Walt noticed they especially liked climbing and leaping from one stuffed animal head to another, sniffing, crawling in mouths, and sitting on top of the antlers cleaning themselves. They really were acrobatic.

The men decided to talk about the arc of the movie first. Once again Brent took charge of the discussion.

"The way I see it, this story of mine has all the drama it needs just by changing the names and telling it like it happened. Did you read my synopsis?"

JJ didn't say anything. Every time Brent spoke, JJ frowned. Brent noticed and smiled at him, enjoying JJ's discomfort.

"That's one way to see the story," said Walt, "But why not juice it up a little, add subplots and interactions? Brent, your synopsis indicates that this was simply a power play between bad neighbors. There was very little actual interaction between the sides. The hippies were bad neighbors for sure. The ranchers, for their part, were vindictive and inflexible. It was mainly a simmering passive dispute, until the sheriff got involved with the evictions 9 months after the hippies moved in with their buses and parties and the general chaos that alarmed the community."

"I disagree. Keep it simple. I've done the work for you. Nothing could be better here than the truth," said Brent.

"I think it needs more. What do you say JJ?" said Walt.

"I think it needs more," said JJ. "What about an anti Vietnam war angle? The rancher has a son who is serving. The hippies have a former soldier, now disillusioned?"

"That never happened," insisted Brent.

JJ raised his hand.

"What about a love angle between the two sides? The rancher's daughter falls in love with a hippie? A doomed Romeo and Juliet angle?"

"Unacceptable, *Julien.*" Brent crossed his arms.

JJ bristled, "It's JJ. I told you."

"Oops, sorry. Heh heh."

Kato was fidgeting in his chair next to Walt, "I have a great idea to add."

"No," said Brent. He pointed at Kato. "Absolutely not. This is between us writers."

Walt chimed in, "I agree with Brent 100%. Sorry Kato. No offense. I'm sure you have what it takes, but the three of us need to get our working dynamic going. We can't waste time."

JJ looked over and saw that this interaction bothered Brent. He saw his chance to get back at Brent!

"I think we should give Kato a chance," said JJ, smiling in triumph.

"No," said Walt.

"Hell no," said Brent.

"What harm could it do?" said J.J.

"No," said Walt. "Brent is right."

There was silence.

"Why don't you just hear my idea? If you don't like it, then I'll back out," said Kato.

More silence. Then JJ said, "Come on. Just this once."

"I don't like it," said Walt.

Brent shook his head no.

"Go for it Kato," said J.J.

"Here's my idea," said Kato, putting his elbows on the table and leaning forward. "What if one of the tactics the rancher uses is to try to buy out the hippies' mortgage, and get them foreclosed and tossed off the land?"

More silence, then Walt said "What do you think, Brent?"

Brent hesitated, and said "It...It's actually not a bad idea. It could work within the framework of the historical facts."

Kato beamed. "See. That wasn't so bad."

"Let's talk about some of the main characters, and get some names."

They spent the next hour talking over the broad strokes of the plot and naming the characters. Kato joined in for the entire time. There was no stopping him. The camel's nose was under the tent. They took a break at 10am.

When they came back, Kato set out a line of coke on a plate, snorted it, and said: "Want a toot? Best coke in the world."

They all declined.

"Your loss," he said and did another line. "Wooeeee, that was good."

It soon became clear that Kato on coke had a vastly more outrageous take on how the story should be told.

First he suggested that there should be CIA infiltration of the hippies. Everyone voted it down. Next he suggested that there should be supernatural forces at work. Everyone voted it down. But Kato dominated the conversation. It went on and on in this manner, from Kato suggesting zombies to Kato suggesting Alien abduction. By lunchtime, they were all exhausted by Kato's frantic energy. They had accomplished next to nothing.

"What are you making us for lunch, Kato? I'm starved," demanded Brent.

"I'm not making lunch. I'm not making dinner. I'm not making anything. Make it yourself. I'm going to write this screenplay, with or without you." Walt, JJ and Brent sat there, dumbfounded.

"Kato, you should go back home, if you're not going to cook and help us. Worse, you've become a distraction," said Brent.

"You go home," said Kato. "Filippo Giardia is my uncle. He sent me here to keep you on track. That's what I'm doing. If you guys can't write this, I can. I'll go home when my uncle tells me to go home. Nobody gets to order me around. Not you. And not Irv Gottlieb for that matter."

Brent got up. He looked at Kato and shook his head. He scowled at JJ. He went to the kitchen and rummaged around the pantry and came up with a loaf of bread and some peanut butter and jelly. He made himself a sandwich, leaving the plastic bread bag open and everything else laying on the counter. He didn't clean up. He sat on one of the sofas in front of the fireplace.

Walt made himself a sandwich. He didn't clean up either. He left the room in a huff. Then JJ went to the counter with the ferrets in his arms. The ferrets tore into the bread bag, ripping it open and tossing out bread.

"No no my darlings, wait your turn." JJ pulled the ferrets away. They sat and watched.

He pulled two pieces of bread out for himself and made a peanut butter and jelly sandwich. Then he put peanut butter and jelly on one slice of bread and cut it into several small pieces.

"Here you go babies, here's your own sandwich." JJ didn't close up the bread bag or clean up. He went to his room, leaving the ferrets to feast unsupervised on the counter top.

Kato paid no attention. He was at the table, furiously typing on his laptop the whole time, a wild grin on his face. A bottle of powdered cocaine sat next to the laptop.

Chapter 8

The demoralized crew assembled around 3pm to give it another try. Kato was still hard at work.

"I have it," announced Kato. "This is the best idea yet," said Kato to the group. "The hippies are actually Nazi vampires, posing as hippies. The LSD allows them to come out during the day, so the story centers on the ranchers trying to get the FBI to seize the hippies' LSD, so they can kill them or burn them with sunlight. Cool movie, huh?"

"I hate it," said Brent.

"No," said Walt.

JJ ignored everyone. He was still mad at Brent. He put his noise canceling headphones on and started playing a video game on his cell phone. The ferrets climbed onto his lap. They crawled through his clothing, or frolicked around the table. Meanwhile Walt, Brent and Kato argued some more. Walt and Brent rejected everything Kato offered. They couldn't shut him up. He was too antic, too amped up to control.

"I can't take any more of this," Brent announced. "Let's vote. I say Kato is off the team. Who is with me?"

"Sorry Kato," said Walt. "It's for the best. I agree. We gave you a try. It didn't work out."

Brent looked at JJ, who was lost in his game and hadn't heard a word. Brent was not a man who accepted being ignored.

Brent asked JJ. "What about you JJ?"

JJ didn't respond. He was smiling at something in his video game. "JJ." No response.

"JJ! JJ are you there?" Nothing.

Brent reached over and grabbed for JJ's noise canceling headphones. That was a big mistake. All hell broke loose.

One ferret, with fur sticking out all over its body in hackles, stood on the table, snarled viciously and lunged for Brent's hand, barely missing it. Brent leaped back out of his chair and nearly fell over. The second ferret leaped out of JJ's shirt and took a defensive position next to the first ferret, snarling and hissing and challenging anyone. Walt and Kato leaped out of the way.

JJ just sat there. He kept playing his game. He put one finger out and gently stroked one of the ferrets, which did nothing to calm it down. The

Flying Ferretinis were laser focused on Brent, hissing, showing their teeth, and ready to attack.

After several long seconds, JJ slowly took off his headphones, and looked sweetly at Brent and said "Yes?"

"That God damned creature attacked me!"

"The Flying Ferretinis are very possessive of my personal space. They are quite attuned to spot and defend me against aggressive behavior. I would say it was...your fault...Brent."

"Unbelievable," snarled Brent, standing up and heading for the door, "You won't get away with this. I'm taking a walk." Brent slammed the door on his way out. The ferrets hissed at him as he left. JJ cooed to his ferrets. He put them on the floor and headed back to his room. Kato decided he would go to the guest house to work.

Walt's adrenaline was pumping. He got a large glass of water and drank it. Then he headed outside. There were two wooden lawn chairs under the large cottonwood next to the abandoned dog kennels. He sat down. The animal attack had been terrifying, but it was also thrilling. He felt alive, like he had awakened from a long sleep. The adrenaline gave him inspiration for a new way forward to make this movie, Kato included. It was a dangerous idea. It was beyond foolish, but it could work. He now knew he wanted to do this screenwriting job more than ever. He felt buzzed and exhilarated. His plan would work, but it was crazy.

There was just one huge problem with his plan: He needed to get drunk and take drugs to make it work. Walt hadn't taken a drink in 25 years. His world in Bakersfield centered around a stable home life, a stable work life, AA meetings at least once a week, regular calls to his sponsor, and him sponsoring others. It worked for him. He hadn't felt the urge to drink at all for years – until just now.

Walt was certain his own brand of drunken craziness, once so familiar, would easily match Kato's. His will power would dominate the others. Remembering back over 25 years ago during his drunken Hollywood days as a successful screenwriter, he saw himself being able to do it one more time.

This time if he drank, it would be different. He had perspective now. He would stop when he needed to. He could stop. Sure he could. He was grown up. He was changed. He remembered how he used to successfully dominate the creative circles of writers with his will, his wit, his power when he was drinking. It was the best time he had ever had in his life. He could relive those times. He was having those old creative feelings again now, for the first time in decades, and he wanted this heady exhilaration to go on and on. The old Walt was back, and he was better than ever. He could do this, and he could do it while drinking. He wanted it. It was the right thing to do.

But his better angel whispered: *No Walt. It'll be the same, just like when you used to go on a bender and end up in a puddle outside a bar with your pockets turned inside out. You can't do this. You tried. You failed. It ruined you, ruined your first marriage, ruined your work, and ruined your relationship with your kids. You lost it all. You can only do the things you can actually safely do, and drinking, or doing that cocaine you want so much right now isn't one of the things you can safely do. Slow and steady, that's the trick. No excitement. Breathe in, breathe out. Balance. Accept it. You are an incurable alcoholic.*

The other voice disagreed. *I want this so bad. I feel so good right now. I want to get back into the Hollywood world. I belong there. I can do this.*

He was arguing with himself, looking out at the distant blue gray mountains, when a voice behind him said: "Can I sit here with you Walt?"

He turned. It was JJ. Walt looked for the ferrets. He was a bit afraid of them. JJ didn't have the ferrets.

"Sure. Sit down, JJ. It's nice out here." JJ sat in the other chair. They sat in silence. Walt continued arguing with himself. He was definitely leaning towards drinking.

Finally JJ said: "Fucking Brent."

Walt looked over, "He really gets under your skin, doesn't he?"

"He's a bully. People like him have been tormenting me my entire life. I'm sick of it." They sat silently for a while.

Walt answered, "You are right. Brent's a bully, and a blowhard. He's ruthless and successful. But you want to know something?"

"What?"

"He is easy to control. You can actually work with the Brents of this world. I could. You should try."

"Really?"

"Sure. It's simple. Ask yourself, what does Brent really want?"

"Fuck if I know. I don't care."

"The Brents of the world are insecure. Brent wants to be validated, and stroked constantly. He's an insecure narcissist. He's not self-contained like you. He craves attention. You didn't give him that, and because you didn't validate him, he's insecure around you. So, he has to go on the offensive, and put you in your place. By not stroking his ego, you gave him the opportunity to belittle and hurt you. He's good at it. Of course you didn't deserve it. But that's who he is, take it or leave it."

JJ said nothing for a bit, then said, "I guess."

They sat there for a while longer.

"What do you think about Kato, Walt?"

Walt took a deep breath. He was gathering his thoughts, because JJ would not like what he was about to say.

"Kato was your mistake, JJ. That one's on you. You can't blame Brent for Kato."

"What? I didn't...."

"Yes you did. Kato was your mistake," Walt interrupted. "Kato wanted in on the screenwriting. That was obvious. Brent and I said hell no, but you didn't back us up. You left us in the lurch. No, it was obvious that you wanted to needle Brent because he was needling you. Taking Kato's side was childish of you. That's all it took. You uncaged the demon. You turned loose Beetlejuice."

"Beetlejuice?" He paused. "You think I'm responsible?"

"Yes. That was unprofessional. I saw Kato's nature right away, from the first second I met him. You missed it. Kato is bad news from start to finish. I knew plenty of Katos when I was in Hollywood. He's the type you want to steer clear of at all times."

"What are we going to do?" asked J.J.

Walt snorted, "Nothing we can do about it. He's a force of nature at this point. The best we can hope for is that maybe he'll crash and lose interest in the project."

JJ sighed. He didn't say anything for a while. "Damn. What a mess. You know Walt, if this project had just been you and me, I think we could have easily taken it on, and collaborated well on it".

Walt looked at the younger man. "I think you're right. I think we could have easily written this movie together."

"Why did you leave Hollywood, Walt?"

Walt paused, deciding how much personal information to share.

"I left because I'm an alcoholic. I crashed and burned and ruined everything good in my life, and on the way down I ruined everyone else's life around me. You would not have liked me in those days. Not one bit. You know, JJ. You remind me a bit of myself. You're an angry man. I was once an angry young man too."

JJ stood up, greatly offended.

"Fuck you. I'm nothing like you. Not even close. I'm not a drunk. I don't take drugs. Don't compare yourself to me. You don't know me."

Walt looked at JJ with compassion in his sad, hound dog eyes. "You're right, JJ. I'm sorry. You're nothing like me."

"Damn straight." JJ walked away.

And at that moment, Walt's craving for alcohol and drugs simply vanished. The dark spell of compulsion was unexpectedly broken. Just like that, it was gone. He took in a breath, and let out a spontaneous sob that was made up of a little bit of self pity and a huge amount of relief. *Not today. I'm not gonna drink today. I won. Just today. Thank God. I made it. I'm not gonna ruin my life, not today. I was so close, but I'm gonna make it through. Oh Bless this day.*

Walt also realized that he was not going to make this movie. He was ok with it. Walking away was the correct path. He would go back to his ordered, calm life and teach college English in Bakersfield. He felt good. He was looking at the distant hills feeling grateful when he heard sudden angry yelling from back at the lodge. It was Brent yelling, and it sounded bad. Then he heard another voice. It shouted a single word: "No!" That was JJ.

Walt ran for the lodge.

Chapter 9

The voices were coming from upstairs and Walt climbed the stairs at a run. As he reached the inside balcony at the top of the stairs, Kato came in the front door of the lodge and stopped.

The door to the upstairs bedroom was open. Brent was holding his cowboy hat. It had a big chunk missing from the brim. The whole room was a complete mess. There were pillow feathers everywhere, the bedding was torn, Brent's clothes were strewn all over, and the room smelled awful. JJ was backed against a wall, and Brent towered over him. One large hand was a fist, and the other was shoving the damaged cowboy hat in JJ's face.

Walt was amazed: How could two ferrets do this much damage?

"Look what those god damned ferrets did!" screamed Brent. His face was red with rage.

"Get that hat out of my face."

"This hat is a collector's item!"

"Fuck your hat, and fuck you."

"Collectors item!" Brent looked around, "Where are those fucking weasels?"

"Leave them alone. I'll get you a new hat."

Walt tried to diffuse the situation, "Come on guys. Settle down. Settle down. It's just a hat."

Brent wasn't having it, "I'll kill them. I'll kill them."

Brent threw his hat on the bed and crossed the room to his suitcase. He rummaged through it and came out with a revolver and holster. Brent strapped on the old fashioned holster, which dropped to one side Hollywood gunfighter style. At the sight of the revolver Walt fled. Down the stairs he flew, and at the bottom, he stopped. He looked around. Something was different in the room. What was it? Then he saw what it was: The glass case holding the Winchester Rifle was standing open and the big rifle was missing. *And where is Kato? Oh no.*

"Leave my ferrets alone," yelled a desperate JJ.

JJ ran down the stairs just a few steps ahead of Brent.

"Stop!" JJ screamed. "They are my emotional-support animals!"

"They're dead emotional-support weasel meat when I find them! You can scrape them off the floor for emotional support. I'll show you emotional support." Brent was snarling like a ferret himself.

When Brent reached the bottom of the stairs, Kato suddenly stepped out of the pantry and pointed the Winchester at the center of Brent's chest.

"Freeze podner." Brent stopped. His mouth fell wide open. His eyes bulged.

Kato smiled. "I've always wanted to say that. How'd it sound? Did it work for you? Put your gun down on the stairs, Brent. "

Brent didn't move. Kato crossed the big room towards Brent, sighting down the rifle.

"Brent, I'll kill you. I hate animal abusers more than anything. No bluff."

Brent put the revolver on the stairs.

"Good choice. Now step away. All of you. Stand in the middle of the room. Put your hands on your heads and keep 'em there." Brent, JJ and Walt walked to the middle of the room with their hands on their heads.

Kato picked up the revolver. He spun the well-oiled cylinder.

"Nice six shooter, Brent. A real antique. I must say it goes well with my winchester. Hmm. He spun the cylinder again. Shall we play a little Russian roulette later, Brent?" He put the pistol in his waistband.

"Don't hurt anybody Kato," pleaded Walt.

"Shut up. Turn around. Don't face me. Face the fireplace. Don't move."

Kato walked into the kitchen, keeping the rifle ready. Quickly, he ducked into the pantry and came back with a tray and 4 glasses. He pulled out a bottle of whiskey and poured four shots. He added a bit of water and stirred them with a long spoon.

"Now turn around." They turned around, hands on heads.

"Now walk over to the table, real slow, and take your places." They walked over. Brent sat at the head in his place. JJ and Walt sat on either side.

"Put your hands on the table. Don't move them." They did it. Kato took out his vial of coke, stuck a fingernail inside and sniffed some into each nostril.

"Ahhh. That's better."

Still pointing the Winchester at one and then another, Kato smiled crazily.

"Now we're gonna just chill the fuck out, especially you," he said, pointing the rifle at Brent.

"We're gonna sit here, calmly. We're all gonna have us a little drink together, and we're all gonna just CHILL....THE....FUCK....OUT!"

He walked over to the counter, picked up the tray with glasses and came to the table. He set a glass in front of each of the three hostages. He took a fourth glass and stood by the sink. With the rifle in one hand and his glass held up in the other he said: "This is the good stuff, the single malt. Now drink! Cheers!" He drained his drink and laughed maniacally.

Brent picked up his glass and downed it in two gulps. JJ took a sip. Walt left his glass on the table. Kato noticed. He set his glass down and pointed the rifle at Walt.

"Drink up Walt. Everybody drinks."

"I don't drink."

"You do today."

"No. I can't drink that."

"Why?"

Walt paused. "I'm an alcoholic."

Kato found this hilarious. He moved the rifle to cover Walt. Smiling, he said, "You're worried about alcoholism now, in the last minute of your life, with this gun pointed at your face?"

"I'm not drinking that," said Walt, shaking his head, staring down the barrel of the Winchester.

Kato stared back. Then he shrugged his shoulders, walked to the sink, and filled a glass full of water. He put the water in front of Walt. He took Walt's whiskey glass and set it down in front of Brent.

"You need a refill, Brent. Drink up." Brent drank it.

Walt's tongue and mouth were dry from adrenaline. He drank half the water in one long pull.

"Now that we've taken a last drink, let's talk about what's gonna happen. First of all, I really don't like animal cruelty, Brent. That's not cool, not at all."

Kato sat at the end of the table opposite Brent. He put the rifle on the table and took out the pistol and held it up. Brent appeared a bit unsteady. The two drinks were affecting him.

"I'm gonna write this screenplay all by myself. I don't need any of you. You're all losers. You're all useless. But I don't want any distractions. What am I gonna do?" Kato paused.

"What I'm thinking is this: I'm gonna shoot the two of you with Brent's six-gun." He pointed Brent's pistol at JJ, and then at Walt.

"Then, after that, I'm gonna shoot Brent with the big rifle. And put Brent's pistol back in his dead hand. I'll fire three rounds towards where I was standing when I shot Brent and it'll look like self defense, plain and simple. My story will be that there was this big argument between JJ and Brent over the Flying Ferretinis – that's true -- Brent pulled a gun – that's true also -- things got out of hand and he killed JJ and Walt and I shot it out with Brent. Of course, I'm the only one left alive to tell the story. Pretty neat huh? Well, except for the Flying Ferretinis. I'll take care of them. I like them. You really shouldn't have threatened them, Brent. That was uncalled for. Anyway, that's what I'm thinking. But, I'm still undecided. It would be a rather permanent decision." He giggled, his coked up eyes addled in an imaginary elsewhere while he spoke.

Brent was weaving more in his seat, "My hat. My hat," he slurred.

"Please Kato," whispered JJ.

"Let us go," said Walt. Just then Kato's laptop chimed. He looked at his watch.

"Oh shit. I forgot about Irv's zoom call. Damn, damn, damn."

He put the rifle on the floor. He was suddenly not so sure of himself.

"We're going to take his call. I'm going to be pointing this pistol at you underneath the table. We're going to have a quick and friendly chat with Irv. Don't even think of warning him. If you do, I'll cut the connection, and shoot you. That will make my mind up for certain. So smile for Irv. We're a group of friends having a friendly drink. Smile. Tell Irv everything is terrific, the screenplay is making great progress."

"Terrific," slurred Brent, swaying in his seat, "I'm terrific."

"That's the spirit Brent. Let's see a big smile from you JJ, and you Walt."

JJ grimaced. Walt smiled. Kato opened up the laptop. Irv Gottlieb appeared on the screen. He was in his study.

"Hey fellas! How are you? First full day on the job. I'll bet things are going well, right."

"Teeerific," slurred Brent. "I'm just teeerific."

"Ho ho, ho," said Irv. "It's great to see a creative team coming together, cementing your progress with an after work drink. Letting off a little steam, eh? Oh boy. I remember those days, having an afterwork drink with the crew. Oh man I wish I were with you guys. I envy you."

"I'm teerific," slurred Brent once more.

"Hoo hoo. I'm sure you are Brent. You look swell."

"We're making solid progress, Irv," said Walt mechanically. "Things are going great."

"That's what I want to hear." A phone rang in Irv's office.

"Oh, I have to take this. You guys get back to your party. Take care. Talk to you tomorrow." Irv broke the connection. Kato closed the laptop, walked into the kitchen and unplugged the internet router. They were now completely isolated with no connection to the outside world.

"I'm feeling sleepy," said Brent. He put both hands on the table to steady himself. "I'm going to sleep." He put his big forehead on the table and passed out. His arms flopped down off the table.

Kato put the pistol into his waistband. He picked up the rifle and held it with the muzzle pointing down, away from the men. He picked up the internet router.

"I have a screenplay to write. You won't have to worry about Brent causing you any more trouble. I spiked his drink." He turned towards the door. Then he paused and turned back.

"Don't worry. You two guys are alright. I'm sorry. We're cool. But let me tell you something about Brent. I don't like guys like him. He's a phony. He comes off like this lifelong western rancher, but he has only had his ranch for a few years. Brent comes from LA. He made millions in luxury real estate. He's the realtor who sold Irv his Hollywood mansion. But most of his fortune came from evicting poor renters who live in modest apartment buildings. He's no fucking cowboy. No more than I am. But you guys are alright. Sorry." Kato opened his coke vial, took another hit, gathered the rifle and the router and walked out the door.

Chapter 10

As soon as Kato was inside the guest house, JJ jumped up and ran into his room. He whistled and the ferrets ran to him from where they were hiding.

Walt was left sitting at the table in shock. Comatose Brent was on his right. Something was wrong with Brent. His breathing wasn't right. He would breathe in a little, then he would stop, his head would shake a bit, and after a couple of seconds he would take another little breath.

"JJ," Walt shouted. "Come here. Brent's having trouble breathing. Help me." He stood and lifted Brent's head off the table, and sat him up in the heavy wrought iron chair. Brent's head lolled to the side. His breathing was still labored. JJ ignored Walt.

"JJ!" Walt yelled. "Get your ass out here! The man is in trouble!"

JJ poked his head out his bedroom door. He had a terrified look on his face.

"Help me. We need to get him to the couch. He's not breathing right."

JJ looked panicked.

"Help me."

"No. Kato is going to kill us. He's killed before. He's out of control. He's on drugs."

"Just help me move him. I can't do it on my own. It'll just take a minute."

JJ reluctantly came over.

"He's a maniac."

"Yeah. Help me drag the chair over to the couch."

Together, holding Brent in the chair, they dragged him across the flagstone floor. The iron chair legs made a horrible screeching sound against the floor. The two men got Brent next to the couch and flopped him down.

"Help me turn him on his side. That way if he vomits, he won't suffocate." They turned him and JJ ran back into the bedroom.

Brent was now taking shallow, irregular breaths, and gasping in between. *Maybe he has a CPAP machine,* thought Walt. He ran upstairs. While he was looking at Brent's stuff, he heard JJ run out to his car. A few seconds later, the car sped off down the road.

There was no CPAP machine. Walt came downstairs. He made the decision to stay up and watch Brent. Walt went into his room, packed his bags, and put them by the front door. He grabbed a Batman pillow and a spaceship children's blanket, and set himself up on the couch opposite Brent.

The irony of this situation, and the foolish choice he was making to try to save Brent wasn't lost on Walt. Once again, he remembered that life was all about choices. Back when he was an active drunk, he could have chosen not to drink. He could have chosen not to ruin his first marriage, his relationship with his kids, his career, and all his friendships. But he made the choice to drink, even if it was a compulsion, and he ruined his life and he hurt everyone else. His recklessness and his shocking selfishness ran his life into the ground. It was a choice.

Now, after 25 years of making general amends and sincere reparations, and just trying to be a better man in the world, here he was every bit as reckless as he once was, risking his life. Just across the parking lot sat a fully armed, coked out hair trigger sociopath, a truly dangerous man.

And why was Walt trying to save detestable Brent? Why was he trying to save this man who tossed thousands of people on the street and lost not a minute of sleep, no doubt by telling himself that the people he evicted brought it all on themselves? Brent Gardner was a wretch who washed his hands of human suffering. He was a man who wouldn't piss on your leg if your pants were on fire.

And here was Walt, making a fateful choice, choosing a suicidal risk. No blaming booze this time. He knew full well what he was doing. He knew the correct choice was to run for his life like JJ, to not be stubborn and self destructive. But at this moment, it didn't matter to him. Why? Because Walt realized he was feeling more alive and awake and energized than he had at any time in the last 25 years. He was exhilarated, chasing a high he hadn't felt for decades. The danger didn't matter. The danger was the point, and it felt just right. He clearly knew this charity towards Brent was as selfish as anything he did back in the old days. He knew he wasn't noble. He knew he hadn't changed a bit, and he never would. He just wasn't drinking.

His wife would be devastated if Kato suddenly got writer's block and shot Walt in a pique of frustration. Even this didn't matter to Walt. He knew what he was going to try to keep feeling this exhilaration alive. *Screw it. I'm going to save Brent.* So he sat listening to Brent's labored breathing. About 1 am, Brent's breathing became regular, and it was safe for Walt to rest. He looked out the window. All the lights were still on in the guest house. Walt was exhausted. He fell asleep.

Chapter 11

Early Sunday morning

It was dark when Walt woke to noises coming from upstairs. Brent was no longer on the couch. *Brent must be packing,* thought Walt, with a yawn. He sat up, feeling old and groggy. He looked at his watch. It was 4:00 am. Brent came tromping down the stairs, his cowboy hat on his head. It looked like the hat of a cowboy movie ne'er do well, a big chunk bitten out of the side. He stopped next to the couch where Walt sat, wrapped in the children's blanket.

"How do you feel?" asked Walt.

"Great. Why shouldn't I? You look like shit."

"Kato drugged you, and it seemed like you might stop breathing so I watched you half the night."

Brent snorted in derision, "Nah. I was fine. You were wrong. You didn't have to do that. It wasn't necessary."

"It seemed necessary."

Brent sniffed. "Nah. I remember Kato got my pistol. We need to get it back. What's the plan? How are we going to get my gun?"

"You're insane."

"He can't have my gun. A man needs his gun."

"Stop. Please. Cut the phony wild west pioneer horse shit. To hell with your gun. I don't know how much you remember from last night, but we nearly all got shot as victims of Kato's perfect crime. If Irv hadn't called and interrupted Kato, we might all be dead now. You're not getting your gun back." They sat there silently.

Brent spoke, "You know, Walt, if it had just been the two of us writing this screenplay, without that dork JJ, and without that fucking Kato, the two of us could have written this screenplay. We would have gotten along just fine."

"Yeah. You may be right Brent. If it had been just the two of us, I think we would have gotten along. I think you're right. We would have written it."

Brent stood and spoke.

"So let's do it! Come on Walt. Let's drive up to my ranch. No distractions. No dork JJ. No Kato. We can do it! Let's go! We've got this."

Walt shook his head, "I'm done. My nerves are shot. I'm through. I can't do it. I won't do it. No screenplay for me."

Brent sneered and picked up his bags, "You're a coward, Walt. That's what you are." He paused to let that sink in.

"What's worse, Walt, is you're a failure." Brent stretched out the word failure. "I can smell failure all over you. That's all you are, a failure."

Walt felt his blood boil as Brent headed for the door. There were a lot of things he could have said, but what he said was:

"I hope Kato doesn't shoot you in the back as you walk to your truck, just like he promised."

As Brent approached the door to leave, Walt stood up and said, "When you were knocked out, Kato said a ton of bad shit about you. He really hates you, you're lucky you're alive. He wanted to shoot you right after he drugged you. I talked him out of it. But I don't expect any thanks from you. He told us you're the farthest thing from a real cowboy, and he told us how you made your money in LA ruining poor people."

"So what?" said Brent. "I made an honest living. I was successful."

"Well, you might not be so successful today. Kato told us what he planned to do with you today. He said he was going to strip you naked down to your boots. He said he was going to give you a running head start into the desert, and then hunt you down like an animal."

Brent was suddenly worried. "No. He wouldn't." He looked around. "Why are you still here?"

"I stayed to save your life."

Brent didn't appear to hear. He was worried enough to find the light switch. He switched off the lights inside the lodge.

Walt saw the surge of real panic in Brent. "Good idea turning out the lights. It makes it harder for Kato to see us here. You should hear the rest of what Kato said."

"There's more?"

"Oh yeah. He talked about tying you naked on the bed, putting peanut butter and jelly on your nuts, and letting those ferrets chew 'em off. He kept repeating that idea. He sure sounded determined to do it. He wants to see you suffer."

Brent turned pale, "That devil."

Walt was only getting warmed up.

"He talked about chaining you naked in the dog kennels and making you live on dog food out of a bowl. Funny how all Kato's ideas had you naked. I'm sure by now he's come up with some new plans since last night. You know how active his imagination is. What I'm telling you is you're not safe going out that front door. He's got special plans in store for you. He's waiting for you – right now."

Brent was paralyzed. "What are we going to do?"

"We? Not me. I'm not going out that door with you. I don't want to get shot because Kato hates your guts."

"What should I do?"

"Well, both doors open onto the porch and then you have a very deadly 60 yard dash to your truck. Or, you could take off on foot into the desert. It's 40 miles to the nearest road. You could make it."

Brent couldn't move. Walt paused, and spoke, "Or, there is a little window in the kids' room. You could squeeze out and sneak around the lodge. After you sneak around the building it's only about 15 yards to your truck. It's still dark. He might not see you."

"Let's do it. I'll go out the window."

They took Brent's bags, and went into the kids' room. Brent opened the tiny window. He threw his bags out first. Then he tried to see if he could go out feet first. There was no way. He was too overweight to get his legs up.

"You'll have to go out head first."

Brent nodded. He took off his hat, and put it on the bunk bed. By going sideways he just got his shoulders through the window, but his big belly was holding him up.

"Help me."

With pleasure. On behalf of all the abused renters everywhere in Los Angeles, I am now forcibly evicting one asshole Brent Gardner by involuntary defenestration. Look out below!

Walt lifted Brent's legs and made ready to shove. "On three, suck in your gut Brent. I'll push. One, two, three!"

Walt pushed as hard as he could and Brent went sliding through the window easily and flew out, landing with a loud thud, a grunt, an ugh, and a long painful "Owwwwwww."

Walt leaned out the window.

"Go Brent, go! You made too much noise. Kato heard you! I heard his door opening! He's coming!"

"My hat!"

Walt pretended to look for the hat. "I can't find it. No time! Hurry! Go! Go!" Brent scuttled away around the building.

Walt picked up Brent's hat. He walked to the front window to watch. In a few moments he saw Brent zig zagging ninja-style across the parking lot. Brent threw his bags in the truck, dove into the driver's seat and seconds later he peeled out of the parking lot.

That was fun.

Walt picked up his bags. He put Brent's cowboy hat on his head and stepped out onto the porch. He paused. All the lights were on in Kato's guest house. He looked around the countryside. A coyote howled in the far distance, and there was a glimmer of dawn in the east. Otherwise it was just him alone with a million stars outside in the perfectly clear night.

It was cold, like it was every night, even now during the late summer. There was no wind. He looked out at the gray mountains in the far distance. He took in a deep breath, and stood in the awesome silence and emptiness. He wondered in awe at the stark simple beauty of the Oregon high desert. It was easy to understand how a person could feel close to God here. At the same time it was unbearably lonely, an inhospitable, pitiless wilderness, and so terribly isolated. Walt realized that it was a place far from the rules and norms of civilization. Societal constraints were only an illusion here. They didn't matter. With no rules, a place like this could loosen any inhibitions. This is cabin fever country.

He walked off the porch and into the parking lot. He stopped and looked towards the guest house. He adjusted Brent's cowboy hat on his head, pulling it down a bit in front and a little off to one side, outlaw style.

He looked around. His mind suddenly filled with questions he wanted to ask Kato about himself. He started walking towards Kato's cottage, but then he stopped, when he thought of his wife, and how she would feel if he got himself stupidly killed. Kato was probably crashing right about now. Walt shivered as he stood for another half a minute in the cold, clear air. Then he walked to his old Subaru, opened the back, put his bags in, and slowly drove away.

Chapter 12

One day later

"Mr. Gardner is angry. Something happened to him down in Oregon, so be careful," said Javier Martinez, the ranch manager at Brent Gardner's Evictus Ranch. He shook his finger back and forth at the two summer ranch interns from Los Angeles, Carlo Berkino and Jonah Wilsky, who stood shivering in the pre-dawn cold, despite their wool coats. They were in the parking lot in front of the bull barn. A diesel pickup truck idled nearby. A stock trailer was attached to it.

"Why do you want us to go with him?" asked Carlo, one of the summer interns. His parents owned apartment buildings in L.A. Gardner used to collect rents for them, and the adults had remained friends with 'Maximize your rent with Brent' after he retired to Montana. The family connection is why Carlo landed this summer ranch internship for himself and his buddy Jonah.

"Why us? We don't know anything about bulls. I'm afraid of them."

"Don't worry about it," assured Javier. "You won't be handling the bull. You are just going along to keep Mr. Gardner company. It's a couple hour drive. The Comstock Ranch will unload the bull they are buying when you get there."

Ten minutes later they were on the road. Carlo sat in the front next to a sullen and silent Brent Gardner. Jonah sat in the back seat of the truck. The boys immediately sensed that something was definitely off with the normally affable Brent. For one thing, he wasn't wearing his usual cowboy hat. He never went anywhere without that hat. It was dark, and Brent drove fast over the bumpy roads, irritating the bull in the trailer. During the entire ride, Brent fumed and scowled. The boys knew better than to say anything.

The Comstock Ranch unloaded the bull without any problems. Brent started driving the return trip home. When they reached the first town, Brent pulled into the parking lot of a tiny restaurant attached to the town's only gas station. There were several other dusty pickup trucks there.

"Pit stop for breakfast," muttered Brent. He slammed his door without waiting for a response. The boys hung back and followed him into the diner.

Over pancakes and eggs, Brent seemed to relax a little, so Carlo decided to try to break the ice.

"Mr. Gardner, I thought you were supposed to be in Oregon for a month. Did something happen?"

Carlo regretted his words immediately, when Brent balled his fists suddenly, and gave him a fierce look. Then Brent turned away and went back to his brooding. They all sat in silence for several minutes.

Brent shook his big head. "It all went wrong. It all went wrong. That God damned Kato." said Brent softly.

"What happened?" asked Jonah.

"There were three of us screenwriters in Oregon to write the movie. We were supposed to be all alone for a month. The only other person there was this crazy punk named Kato Worsen. Us three writers were trying to find our way as a team of writers when this punk started doing lines of coke. He ruined everything."

Carlo and Jonah gave each other a knowing look. Coincidentally they knew about Kato. Both came from wealthy Beverly Hills families. Both were going to UCLA in the fall. Kato was a legendary screw up from Beverly Hills, eight years older than Carlo and Jonah. They had heard plenty of Kato stories.

"How did Kato end up there?" said Carlo.

"You know Kato?"

Both boys emphatically shook their heads. "No no. We don't know him. We've never met him. But we've both heard stories. He is from Beverly Hills, just like us."

Brent nodded. "Somebody is going to take him out someday, and I will be the first to rejoice. The only reason he was with the screenwriters is because his uncle is the head of the studio producing the movie we were working on."

"Oh. That explains why he was there. So what happened in Oregon?" said Carlo.

"What happened is Kato started doing coke. Lots of it. He butted in on the writing project. Then he went completely crazy. He kidnapped the three of us at gunpoint and tied us up. He got my hat. He told us he was going to shoot us. He said he was going torture us first."

"Torture?"

"Yeah. We were tied up to our chairs. He walked around waving this old Winchester rifle in our faces. He took my sidearm too. Damn it. He got the drop on me, or I would have blown his punk ass away."

"Wow."

Brent was warming to his storytelling. "So there I was, tied up and helpless, with no chance to escape, with two sniveling cowardly screenwriters to protect. Those guys were totally useless. It was all up to me. Kato told us he was going to put us in these dog cages out back. He was going to put rattlesnakes in the cages, or rats, or skunks, or whatever animals he could catch. I laughed and told him to his face that I swore I was going to kill him with my bare hands if I ever got loose. He was deranged. He said he was going to stake us outside naked, and put peanut butter on our testicles and let the wild ferrets and ants chew on our gonads. Sick shit. Before that he said he was maybe thinking of stripping us naked and hunting us in the desert."

"Unbelievable. How did you escape?"

"It was my quick thinking. He left us in the main house, to go sleep, or get more drugs or something. I don't know. He left. That is when I made my move. He didn't know I had a secret knife in my boot. I cut myself loose, then I freed the others. The other two screenwriters were terrified. They were curled up on the floor, going crazy with panic. Like I said, they were both totally useless."

"But not you."

"No. I wasn't afraid. Not at all. I was just pissed. I knew Kato was a punk. So I walked outside, unarmed, and stood there while the two other screenwriters made their getaways. I called him out."

"Wow."

"Yep. That's what I did. I called him out all right, but he wouldn't face me. Then I dared him to shoot me in the back as I walked away to my truck. Nothing happened, because he is a yellow punk."

"You didn't call the police?"

"Nah. I knew it would embarrass the studio. I'm loyal, so I kept quiet. I saved the lives of the other two guys. That is for sure, but did they ever call me up and thank me? No. Not a single God damned word of thanks from either of them. Can you believe their ingratitude?"

"They should have thanked you," said Carlo.

"What a story," said Jonah.

Brent nodded and poured himself some more coffee. "Yep. Hell of a story. Boy, I do miss my hat though. That hurts the most. A man needs his hat."

Chapter 13

Two weeks later, Brent received this letter

From: Karboy and Klench, Attorneys at law
13984 Wilshire Boulevard, suite 2321
Los Angeles California

To: Mr. Brent Gardner, Evictus Ranch
P.O Box 324
Settlers Pass Montana

CC: Julien Pinkus, Walter Journey

RE: Your demand letter for compensation

Dear Mr. Gardner:
    I represent Mr. Filipo Giardia, TransPacific Partners Studios, and Mr. Irving Gottlieb. We are in receipt of your demand for additional compensation for your two days of screenwriting. We are well aware that your two days in Oregon did not result in a single word of screenplay. As far as we are concerned, you are in total breach of contract. The studio has decided to cancel the "When the Love Left" movie project entirely. There will be no movie.
    Mr. Giardia and the studio would like to put this matter behind them. Therefore, we are offering you three screenwriters the following settlement:
    The studio will pay each of you $35,000 in exchange for your signature on the enclosed confidentiality agreement and covenant not to disclose any of the events that took place during your short stay in Oregon. This confidentiality explicitly covers anything allegedly said or allegedly done by Mr. Kato Worsen. Any such allegations about his conduct are hereby strenuously and explicitly denied.
    Let me point out two benefits that might help the three of you decide whether to take this offer besides the generosity of the settlement itself.
    First, signing the confidentiality agreement and accepting the settlement will result in you being considered -- without prejudice -- for other projects in the future. For example, Mr. Giardia has expressed a keen

willingness to examine three of Julien Pinkus' project proposals, should Mr. Pinkus sign.

Second, If you sign, the studio will not pursue a breach of contract action against each of you, which would ruin your reputations in the movie business. The studio will also honor its share of the confidentiality agreement. The studio will not disclose or gossip about how you utterly failed to complete your contractual assignment.

Mr. Gardner, we deny your demand for additional compensation of $18,000 to compensate you for the cost of replacing your cowboy hat that was once supposedly owned and worn by movie cowboy Roy Rogers. We also deny your claim for the loss of "Richard Boone's six-shooter," allegedly used in the TV series "Have Gun Will Travel." A thorough search of the Love Dog Ranch turned up no such cowboy hat or revolver. We have no proof that these items were ever at the ranch. No reasonable person would ever take such an unwise risk of losing valuable collector's items.

We look forward to receiving your signed confidentiality agreements and to working with you in the future.

Very Truly Yours, S/ Ronald Klench,

PART 2
CAINE ENABLED

"Sous chaque fortune, il y a un crime."
Under every fortune, there is a crime.
   French proverb

Moth: You are a gentleman and a gamester, Sir.
Armado: I confess both: They are both the varnish of a complete man.
   Shakespeare, Love's Labor's Lost

Chapter 1

   "What's wrong with you Kato?" yelled Phil Giardia, shaking his fist at his nephew Kato Worsen. "I gave you every break and advantage in life. I cut you slack and I defended your bad behavior. Irv says I should have set boundaries like he did. It's my fault. I've been such a fool. You ruin everything you touch. Everything!" Phil was standing next to his Louis XIV chair in the gilded, ornate 'Hall of Mirrors' room in his Hollywood mansion.
   Kato was looking worn out, and badly in need of a good night's sleep. He sat on the couch and waited for the barrage to continue. Kato knew he was there for an ass chewing. There was no getting out of it this time.
   Phil was normally cool, calm and friendly, but not this time. Uncle Phil was furious.
   "You threatened to murder the screenwriters! You pointed a rifle at them."
   "You kind of had to be there. Brent was going to murder innocent animals."
   "I had to pay them over $100,000 to buy their silence and save your sorry ass."
   "You overpaid. I think they would have settled for less."
   "You think this is a joke? Unbelievable! So you were going to tie Brent naked, and let weasels chew on his balls?"
   "That never happened. No. I deny that. No. That's a lie."
   "But you don't deny threatening to kill them all at gunpoint?"

"Well, I can see how some people might misinterpret things. But it wasn't that bad. You really had to be there. It made sense if you look at the gestalt of the moment." Kato dodged around the point, slippery and irresponsible.

"And that so-called screenplay you wrote! Irv read some of it. He said it was Gibberish. 200 monkeys playing on 200 typewriters would have written a better film."

Kato's mouth opened with a surprised look of wounded pride.

"Now that really stings, Uncle Phil. I'm deeply hurt. That comment was uncalled for. I put a ton of my best work into that screenplay. You should read it yourself."

"I trust Irv. He said it was garbage, so it's garbage. He hated every last word of it, so I hate it too. He called it 'the worst screenplay ever.' That's a quote."

Kato turned red with anger.

Phil suddenly let out a moan of pain. He stood there for a second, unsteady on his feet. Then he lay down on the floor and rolled. He clutched his left arm. "Owwww."

"Something wrong, uncle dear?" said Kato mildly, his face still red with suppressed rage.

"Do you like how you feel right now better than you like my screenplay? How would you compare the two experiences?"

"Arrrrrrrrrr!"

"Ok. Are we playing twenty questions then? You're giving me a hint? You're grabbing your arm. Ok. Is the first word Army?"

"Awwwkk!"

"Auckland? Is the answer to this game "The Auckland New Zealand Army? That doesn't make any sense. You need better cues."

Phil passed out. Kato walked over and checked Phil's pulse. He was alive. He dialed 911. While he waited for the 911 operator, he said "You really should treat me better, uncle."

Chapter 2

Darkness, then bright light, then disorientation, and then voices Phil
didn't understand or recognize, then slipping back into darkness again. Over
and over. It went on like this for 2 days. Phil was in a bad way. The doctors
took blood, performed tests, sent probed his arteries, x-rayed, ultrasounded,
then waited.

Darkness, then bright light, disorientation, and then a voice, this time
with a kind face staring into his eyes from a close distance, with a
stethoscope around her neck.

"There you are, Mr. Giardia. Hello. What's your birthday?"

Birthday? Birthday?

"Is it December 3, 1947?"

"That's right. Welcome back." The face turned away, "Mr. Giardia is
awake."

A different face. One Phil knew.

"Hi Phil."

Phil struggled with recognition. "I know you", he said, struggling to
turn his enormous puppet head.

"Yes, you do. It's Lisa."

"Lisa! I know you," again, he managed to turn his tufted bowling ball
of a skull to see her clearly.

Lisa was a vice president in the studio's production wing. She started
out 24 years ago as Phil's secretarial executive assistant. She married him 2
years later, causing the breakup of his second marriage. Phil and Lisa
divorced after less than a year of not-so-wedded bliss, primarily due to Phil's
habitual philandering. It was an amicable breakup, however, and Lisa was by
then such an important part of his production team, that she stayed on and
rose to her present powerful position. She remarried soon after the divorce.
Phil was happy for her, and even walked her down the aisle. After all they
had been through, Lisa was Phil's closest friend and confidant, after Irv, of
course.

"You're back, Phil. Welcome back." Lisa had a sunny, genuine smile for
her boss and friend.

"I'm tired." He shut his eyes. A half hour later he woke up. Lisa was
shaking his shoulder.

"Time to wake up, Phil. The doctor's here."

Phil was more lucid this time, "The doctor's here?"

"Hello, Phil. I'm your cardiologist, Dr. Frind," said a young prematurely bald, busy and serious looking man.

"You've had a heart attack. We did a lot of tests including ..."

"Fugetaboutit. Just give it to me straight Doc. What's the bottom line?"

Dr. Frind looked relieved to be spared from conjuring his not so natural bedside manner.

"Ok. Bottom line, Phil. Heart attack, yes. Damaged heart, yes. Unfortunately, it can't be fixed, and you're not a candidate for a transplant. We can make you comfortable, but you have maybe a couple of months, possibly a year."

"That's it?" Phil was now wide awake. He saw the tubes snaking out of his body, the machines in his ICU room, and the window showing the nurses' station.

"Sorry." Dr Frind looked at Lisa. "I have other patients to see." He left.

"You ok, Phil?" She looked worried. She held his hand.

"I'm in a tough spot. This is it I guess." He paused for a minute, and the old friends sat together. He looked out the window at the LA sky, and thought about his bleak future.

"Has Kato been in to see me?" Phil lolled his broad noggin to get a better view of her.

"No, and he hasn't called either. I did leave messages. Irv has been in every day. He'll be here in an hour."

"Damn. Oh well. Lisa, just get me out of here. If I'm going to die, I want to do it at home."

"Understood. I already have your house set up, nursing care and everything. You can leave tomorrow morning."

"Good." He patted her hand. "That's a relief."

They looked at each other, holding on to time, with urgency. It was clear she was going to miss him.

"I have a crazy idea, Lisa. Let's do something big, crazy big. Let's throw one last big party at my house. Something legendary. I would like that."

"Like the old days? Sure."

"Remember that theme party we threw after the third season of the Fortinelli's? The costume party?"

"You mean where everyone was dressed in mobster and gangster movie formal attire?"

"Yeah. That was fun. Let's do it again. We need to do it soon," said Phil. They sat there for a few minutes, pondering the idea.

"Lisa, Let's call it, 'Phil's Last Party.'"

"Phil's Last Party." She chuckled. "That's a little morbid, but sure, why not. People who know you will get it. Who do you want to invite?"

"How about we try to keep it to the A-list crowd and the executive production people we worked with. But let's make it an open secret in town, so we'll get some surprise crashers. That could be fun. I want a red carpet and a photographer. Let's use the whole downstairs and the entire grounds outside of the house. Live music, of course. Can you get Sting?"

"Maybe. We'll make it the best party. I'll arrange everything."

Phil's face went pale and his bloated cranium tilted backward. He was exhausted.

Chapter 3

Phil's Last Party was well off to an alcohol fueled and raucous start when Irv Gottlieb and his beautiful date stepped out of a rented limousine onto the red carpet. He was one of the last of the guests to arrive. Only one photographer remained at the scene, and he ignored Irv in favor of continuing to talk to a stunning redhead dressed as a 1930's gangster's moll.

"Hey. Take our picture," shouted Irv. He was wearing a tux, and his date was dressed like Carmela Soprano, showing plenty of cleavage and teased blond hair. The photographer looked over, shrugged, snapped a quick photo and went back to his conversation.

The party was packed, and people were getting drunk. The costumes represented every gangster movie and mobster film ever made. The hats on the women were fun and outrageous. A Sting cover band was playing by the pool. Even though it was still only 9pm, several guests had jumped in or had been pushed in, fully clothed, and were frolicking and whooping it up.

"I'm going to go find Phil," said Irv. "Go have some fun, babe."

"Sure Irv," she said, and headed towards the pool.

Irv waded through the guests towards the house, greeting business acquaintances and friends along the way. There was a knot of people trying to get into the house. Irv joined the back of the queue. The man in front of him turned around. Irv noticed he was well dressed, wearing a white tux. He had a sparkling smile, a pleasant face with a large beak nose, but his most noticeable feature was his hair. The man's light brown hair was styled in the manner of a 1980's rock star, in other words, an outrageous mullet.

"Hi. I'm Irv Gottlieb." They shook hands. "You a musician?"

"Sometimes. Hi. I'm Alec Finch. Pleased to meet you, Irv." The man had a very cultured upper crust British accent. He sounded like he belonged in Parliament. In fact, Alec Finch was a British Expatriate with a chronic history of having trouble finding employment, mostly due to his history of aggression and defensive behavior towards anyone critical of his mullet. Finch's only luck staying employed involved jobs where he had to wear a hairnet, mostly fast food establishments.

"I thought you might be, you know, with your haircut."

"Oh yes. I can see how one might think that. It happens quite often. I am a bit of a bass player and a drummer, presently forming a band. But actually, I wear this hairstyle because I'm honoring the world's greatest rock musician, my hero, the extraordinary super star, Rod Stewart."

"I see that now. Yeah. Your hair is Rod Stewart perfect."

"Why thank you, my good man."

"Rod isn't in town tonight, or I am certain he would be here at Phil's party."

"Really! You know Rod Stewart?" exclaimed Finch.

"Of course. Sure I do. Great guy. You must know him, right?"

"Well. Actually we have never met, but I partied with him – or almost with him, one night in Manchester. Rod was upstairs in the hotel. He was partying I hear, and I was in the parking garage of the very same hotel, at the very same time. And I was definitely partying with his limousine driver. So I guess you could say I was pretty close to partying with Rod Stewart."

"That's terrific," said Irv. The line of people to get into the house was moving slowly forward. "Too bad you couldn't meet him tonight."

"My dream." Finch rolled his eyes deliriously, the way an enamored teenage girl might do at a Beatles concert.

What Finch failed to mention was that his aggressive pursuit over the years of Rod Stewart had resulted in three different restraining orders in three different US cities. He was also banned for life from all Rod Stewart concerts in the UK.

As a musician himself, he had no better luck. He thought himself to be a talented bass player who could sing backup. He was actually pretty flashy at playing bass. But on the drums, his erratic pulse made him constantly speed up the tempo regardless of the song.

While developing his latest non-musical project, which he called Socio-Ortho-Genomics, Alec practiced with a 1980's heavy metal band. After a year, they were still practicing in a member's basement, and had yet to book a gig.

"What do you do for a living, Alec?" asked Irv.

"I am an international motivational speaker, also a personal trainer and coach. I have developed a personal growth potential methodology I call Socio-Ortho-Genomics."

Finch developed Socio-ortho-genomics out of his twisted, seething anger. Over years of continual failure, Finch had become increasingly bitter at the world for rejecting him as a musician. This fed his own disappointment as well as his hatred of the ubiquitous discrimination directed at men who chose to wear a mullet.

His disappointment at the only employment he could reliably obtain in the "restaurant" industry culminated in his intense hatred of hair nets. His rage soured into an obsession to get even at a world that considered him a laughingstock. He finally channeled this rage into a manifesto, which in time became the aggressive, unethical, toxic and antisocial self-improvement pyramid scheme he called Socio-Ortho-Genomics.

Alec Finch was urged on by friends and fellow members of The Rock Star Hair Fan Club, an international organization of which he was a past president. The members of The Rock Star Hair Fan Club all wore haircuts of 1970's and 1980's big-hair rock bands.

They had spirited disputes over which musicians had the best hair. For example, the current president, Tony Stroob, living in Leeds England, (and the biggest hater of hair nets in the club), was a huge fan of early Motley Crue hair. Unfortunately, with his curly brown hair, wearing a mullet made Tony look like an angry, rabid poodle. Alec Finch disagreed strenuously with Tony and the Motley Crue look. He preferred the elegant rock star hairstyle of Rod Stewart.

Two months ago, Alec Finch launched Socio-Ortho-Genomics In LA. He was ready and eager for the chance to get rich and get even. He spent every day knocking on doors, and every night crashing parties and events, handing out brochures, and seeking out people who might otherwise be candidates for established programs like Scientology.

Now Irv Gottlieb was in Alec Finch's sights.

"Socio-Ortho-Genomics has the power to transform the world. That is not hyperbole. I truly believe it. Become your true self."

"Oh?"

"Our unique training is designed to unlock a person's fullest potential. I have had an enormous amount of success in the UK. I have helped members of parliament and, of course, the Royal Family."

This was a huge lie. He hadn't been back to Britain for 10 years. He had no contacts with the Royal Family, or anyone, really. If he ever did return to his native country, Rod Stewart was there, ready to sue him for harassment.

Finch continued, "My success has been great, I have been invited to relocate to LA, to help people here become their truest version of themselves."

Alec took a brochure out of his inner pocket and handed it to Irv. Irv put it in his pocket without looking at it. Irv had seen the guest list. Alec Finch was definitely not an invited guest. *So what?* Irv thought. *It's a fun party. Crashers are expected. Let it go.*

Alec Finch had indeed crashed Phil's party after reading about it on a Hollywood gossip website. He rented the tux and climbed over a wall to get onto the mansion grounds, his sole purpose was to hand out brochures, hobnob with celebrities, and try to get a toehold into the celebrity self-improvement market.

"Let me read a bit from my brochure, a story about me from The Times Of London. I quote: 'Alec Finch, is our finest teacher of Socio-Ortho-Genomics. He is one of those rare individuals who come along once in a generation. He is a lion of a man, a sterling patriot of the British Empire, a man of the highest caliber, who has unparalleled wit, intelligence, breeding and discernment. He is a brilliant speaker with a deep, first rate understanding of the human psyche and the modern world. His insights are so keen, he is on a short list for a future knighthood.'"

"Wow," said Irv, "That's high praise." *This guy sure likes to toot his own horn.*

Finch took that comment as encouragement.

"And, here is another quote: 'Many famous actors are enthusiastic about Socio-Ortho-Genomics.'"

"Famous actors? Who said that?" asked Irv incredulously.

"Gary Busey."

"Gary Busey said that? Ohhhhhhh...kay."

The line moved forward. They were almost inside.

"Perhaps I could persuade you to attend a Socio-Ortho-Genomics seminar, Irv? You will unlock your fullest potential. I personally guarantee it. And perhaps I could get your card, Irv?"

Irv ignored his request for a card and looked past Finch, into the house.

"I'll think about it, Alec. Nice to meet you. Have fun at the party."

They were inside. Irv moved off to find Phil, quickly forgetting Alec Finch. *You meet all kinds of screwballs and nuts in Hollywood.* He shook his head and chuckled.

Irv knew that Phil was probably in the Hall of Mirrors, the grand room with floor to ceiling windows, mirrors opposite, and replicas of French art from the 1700's, all designed to look like a famous room in the Palace of Versailles.

Chapter 4

When Irv pushed his way into the Hall of Mirrors, he spotted Phil at the far end. As he got nearer, he saw that part of the room was decorated like the home office scene from the Godfather, where Don Corleone met people during the wedding party. And there was Phil, sitting behind Don Corleone's desk, dressed and made up to look like Marlon Brando in the Godfather, including a pretty good thin mustache. He was receiving people one by one, and staying in Brando character doing it. It was obviously a hit. He was holding forth mightily, and the revelry flowed towards him.

When Irv got close. He saw that despite the makeup and brave, happy face, Phil looked exhausted. Lisa, his ex-wife and vice president of production, stood on one side, a burly security guard in a tux stood on the other side. They were blocking revelers from getting too close to Phil.

Discreetly, the security man held a tube running to a hidden oxygen tank. The mask was hidden inside a plastic drink cup that the security man held. Irv saw Phil nod once to the security guard, and the man brought the cup up to Phil's face. Phil faked taking a drink, while he took in a hit of oxygen.

Phil saw Irv, and shouted above the din of the drunken partiers.

"Irv! I've been waiting for you. Don't go off. I need to talk to you. Clear off everybody. I want to talk to my friend Irv." Irv came up on the other side of the Godfather's desk.

"Good to see you, Phil. Great party. The best ever."

"No kidding. I'm having the time of my life." Phil nodded to the security man, who put the oxygen cup to Phil's face. Phil inhaled, then nodded and the man took the cup away.

"Have you seen Kato, Irv?"

"No, Phil. I just got here."

Phil turned to Lisa. "Is Kato here?" She pulled out her cell phone, hit a speed dial number, and a few seconds later had her answer.

"He's here, out by the pool."

"Get him in here. I want to talk to Irv and Kato together." He took another hit of oxygen. "In fact, Lisa, I think I'm done out here with the crowds. I need to rest. Take me to my room. Go get Kato. Bring Irv and Kato in to see me."

Phil slowly rose from his chair, his security man and Irv holding him up. Phil waved to the buzzing crowd, and in his best Marlon Brando

Godfather imitation said "You give me respect. That's important. For that, I love you all."

With Lisa's help, Phil made it to his ground floor bedroom, where he collapsed on his bed, still dressed in his tuxedo. Lisa fitted him with an oxygen mask.

"I'll go fetch Kato," she said as she was leaving.

A few minutes later, she returned with Kato. Kato looked irritated. He was handsome as always, especially in his black tuxedo. She stood back away from the bed.

Kato smirked. "How are you Uncle?"

"Come closer Kato, you too Irv," Phil whispered very weakly in his Marlon Brando Godfather voice.

They came closer.

"Closer," his voice was even softer.

They were standing above him.

"Closer. Come down." Phil raised one hand and weakly beckoned them to bring their faces down to his level. Their faces were inches from Phil's when, fast as a snake, Phil grabbed Kato by the throat with both hands.

"You betrayed me," he whined in his Marlone Brando voice, while shaking Kato. "I gave you a nice life. I gave you love. I gave you a home like I promised your Mother. I gave you everything. I work all day, and you do nothing."

He let go of Kato's neck and reached for his hand. Kato was shocked and furious, but he didn't pull his hand away.

Phil stopped glaring at Kato. He took Irv's hand with his other hand, and smiled.

"Irv, I'm not going to last long. A month or two or six, maybe a year, but the doctors can't help me. My heart's toast, and I can't get a transplant. You've been a good friend.

"Don't give up hope, Phil."

"I've got something important to tell you, Irv. I want Kato and Lisa to hear it. Irv, I made you the trustee of my entire estate. It's in place now. Talk to my lawyers. They'll explain things. I want you to make great movies. I want you to do charitable work. And I want you to give Kato one last chance to become his true good self, which I have to believe is deep down inside him. One last chance."

"Sure, Irv."

"Kato," said Phil. "Look me in the eye."

"I think you're being a little unfair, a little melodramatic. Come on. You sure it's not your meds talking?" said Kato, who nevertheless looked Phil in the eye, and against his better judgment, moved closer.

"I'm as serious as a head-on car crash, Kato." Phil touched the side of Kato's face, next to his left eye.

"When your Mother was sick, she touched my face like this, and swore in Italian under her breath, and put a Maledetto, a curse on me, if I didn't take care of you. She gave me the evil eye, the malocchio, if I failed to care for you, and she meant it, because she was a witch. And today, Kato, I'm putting that evil eye, that malocchio, back on you. I'm giving you one last chance to succeed in life and become the man of the family. Irv will decide what that chance is. But if you fail, the evil eye will follow you all the way to hell."

Phil muttered something in Italian while tapping the side of Kato's face. He let go of Irv's hand.

"There. It's done. The curse has been cast," said Phil. His engorged head fell back on his pillow; he was exhausted.

"Let me get this straight, Phil," said Irv. "I only have to give Kato one last chance, right? If he fails, I can cut him off forever, banish him, right?"

"Be reasonable, Uncle," interrupted Kato.

"Right, Irv. Kato gets one last chance. You decide what it is. Now please go, all of you. I need to sleep."

Outside in the hall, Lisa went back to the party. Irv caught up with Kato and grabbed him by the arm.

"What? You want to rub it in, humiliate me some more?" said Kato, who stopped and confronted Irv. He towered over the smaller, older man.

"Listen to me Kato. I have words for you. I once loved you like the son I never had. Somewhere inside of you, you know that. We were close when you were a kid. You were a great kid. You were the best. Then you ruined everything. Over the years, Phil and I gave you every chance in life. Modeling, acting, plum jobs in the movie business. You ruined them all. I'm never going to forget that you ruined the screenwriter's retreat a few weeks back. I needed that movie. Now it's gone. That was all your fault. That was a good team of screenwriters, and look what happened. You threatened mass murder. They did nothing to deserve it. They were terrified. Anybody would be. You're out of control. Phil had to buy them off."

Irv was angry as hell. He nodded his head up and down, trying to find the right words.

"Phil wants me to give you one last chance, so I'll do it."

Irv reached into his jacket and brought out the unread brochure for Socio-Ortho-Genomics. He looked at the cover for the first time.

"Here, it says 'Be your true self.' Sure, why not? Take this brochure. Go to this Socio-Ortho-Whatever the fuck it is. But make the most of it because this is your last chance." Irv thrust the brochure into Kato's hands. Kato took it.

"Just give me an excuse and I will cut you off forever. Go ahead, ruin this opportunity too. I dare you. I'll put you on the streets. I loved you once like a son, Kato, but at this point, nothing would give me greater pleasure."

Irv turned and went back into the party, he had to shake his rage. He went to a quiet spot away from the crowds and breathed slowly. In a few minutes his rage lifted. He realized he was ridding himself of the burden of managing Kato. He was clear in his mind and heart that this would be Kato's last chance. If this was the way his relationship with Kato ended, he was okay with it being over.

It was time to stop coddling this miscreant. He would never allow Kato to disappoint him again. Irv drew one more deep breath just in time for the champagne tray to pass before him. Irv smiled and took a glass. He lifted it to the sky. He was grateful for the good fortune of being in control of Phil's empire.

Chapter 5

Kato arrived at the small church in a modest neighborhood in LA. The meeting was downstairs. Handwritten signs pointed the way. An unattended sign-in podium stood near the upstairs entrance. The aroma of old books and dust was in the air.

Kato resented having to be there. He agreed to go, coerced by Irv, as his last chance. Do the workshop or be cut off from Phil's money forever. No more second chances. His impulsive behavior got him into trouble all his life and at his age he had not progressed much past that point.

It was with sneering resistance that Kato set foot in the seminar room and took a seat in the back. Socio-Ortho-Genomics met in the church's Kiddy Care Room, according to the sign above the door. Tiny tables and chairs had been set against the wall along with bins of toys, dolls, and building blocks. There were few windows high up and the room was lit by gently humming fluorescent fixtures. The brown paneling helped keep the room dark.

There were 10-15 attendees. Kato saw the lecturer step to the podium and was pissed off at him. *This is the man I am being forced to listen to?* Kato didn't like it. The ultimatum had been given: get trained or no money. Consequently, he held the man, Alec Finch, in an angry, analytical gaze.

"My name is Alec Finch, and you will never forget me." Finch was wearing a light, cream colored suit, and a white shirt with wide lapels and a cream colored tie.

Look at this guy. Pathetic invented accent. Like that's gonna make me believe your bullshit, pal, you limey shit, Kato thought and shook his head, half listening to the lecture.

You fucking fraud, Kato continued. *Look at that haircut, a bad big hair mullet, like he's supposed to be stylish, like a wanna be Rock and Roll fan...* he chortled. *About 30 years too late for that, jerk.*

Kato bounced his right knee impatiently. He knew he had to make something of this stupid self-help program. Irv meant it. One last chance. He took a deep breath and began to listen.

Alec Finch strutted from side to side holding a microphone as he spoke.

"It is scientifically proven that when a person experiences gratified desire, that person becomes empowered. The sense of power and self-direction is an important factor in bestowing health." The audience murmured.

"It's a proven fact that satisfaction improves health. The more satisfaction, the more health. Why are you sabotaging your own health?" Finch's voice escalated as he looked quizzically out into the audience and shook his head.

"What if I could get you anything in the world you want, your wildest desires? Anything at all." Finch pointed to a man in the front row. "What is your wildest desire?"

The man snickered, then blurted out, "How about a million bucks? That would be nice." The audience laughed.

"Ok. I will get you a million bucks. That's easy," said a smiling Finch.

"How about you?" asked Finch to a woman in the second row.

"I'd like to live in a mansion."

"I can get you a mansion." The audience laughed.

"Who else? You there, what is your wildest desire?"

"A Ferrari sports car, and a private island." The audience laughed. Somebody else raised their hand.

"I want my very own jet, with a bar and catered food," shouted a garishly dressed man in a sing-song voice.

"Who else wants to tell me their wildest desire? I can get you whatever you want." Finch, now at top volume.

He continued pointing around the room randomly and many spoke. Each desire added to the excitement of the evening. Kato didn't speak, though the audience interaction stirred something deep in him. It was a sense of passion that combined his anger and his desire. Kato's rich narcissistic orientation was titillated.

"If this asshole can get everything he wants, I absolutely can do it too." Kato thought, his attention rapt. He hung on Finch's every word and gesture. He listened intently, mostly because his competitive appetite had been ignited.

"Ladies and gentlemen, tonight, I am giving you the unique opportunity to view your world differently." He turned and strutted.

"Capture your world! Own it!" Finch shouted. "Dominate it! Use it!" Finch's voice escalated.

"You see, right now, you're living in fear. There's a voice inside of you saying you shouldn't do this. It's not proper. It's greedy."

"Who feels that? Show of hands." Hands pop up all over the room.

"You see, that's why you're not getting what you want. That little child's voice, that scolded child's voice. The child who took what he wanted and was punished. It's the voice of the defeated kid, the one who wanted more and was told it was a bad thing to want, bad to reach out and get what he wanted."

Finch continued strutting. His head bobbed, the flaky mullet shook.

"Well guess what, you weak idiots? You're not a child anymore. Get what you fucking want! That voice in your head has been poisoning you with lies. That guilty feeling is nonsense. Morality? Ethics? Who cares? This self-defeating poison has been passed down for generations. It's killing you, demeaning your real power, the power of gratified desire, the health giving life blood of existence. Tonight, you will wake up and experience your power, and vitalize your health by fulfilling your desires. It's time to stop demonizing your urge to get what you want, no matter what it is!" Finch's eyes were large black pupils. There was a slight froth on his grinning lips.

"No matter what it is! Do you understand me? Nothing needs to stand in your way. Take it! Take it! You alone are standing in your own way!" Finch was shouting like a money preacher, pink color filling his egg pale face at last.

"You're the one making your world, not mommy and daddy! Wake up!" Finch shouted.

"Are you listening to yourself? You're the one holding yourself back now. There is no mommy and daddy, it's you, you're the one telling yourself that whatever you want needs to be tempered by restrictions. You are thereby diminished! Conscience is an absurd notion. Do you hear what I'm saying now? That voice in your head is not the voice of conscience or reason, it is the voice of defeat holding you back from the very real satisfaction, the real quenching of your soul's desire." Finch grabbed the water, gulped, and set it back on the stand.

"There is no conscience. Real health lies in your choice to be fulfilled. Wake the fuck up. Don't call it greed. It diminishes the full life-giving power of desire. Call it desire. Desire gives us life! Do you understand? It affirms your life! And the more you use it, the more it grows and nourishes your soul."

Finch paused for a moment and stood looking at the audience. The faces were rapt, hanging on his every word.

"I see your faces, you don't believe me! Well you don't have to believe me." His volume rose at the end of each sentence. He was evangelical in his delivery.

Kato's initial snarl had faded. He was engrossed, and his spirit lifted. This mullet headed moron was on to something big. Finch's message resonated within Kato. He was ready to begin simply taking what he wanted. *I'm already doing it!* The doors of his own self-imposed limits opened.

The urge to take whatever he wanted was thumping in his chest. He felt his power to take whatever he wanted. *I don't have to pretend that I don't want whatever I want. I can just take it*, he thought, feeling all impulse control disappearing.

That old cocaine feeling surged through him. The heady powerful thrust of desire pounded in his chest. He stared into the wide black pupils of Finch's face. Kato was feeding on the zeal that emanated from Finch.

What am I waiting for? Until I'm on my deathbed? Why am I pretending that I don't want stuff? There's nothing to stop me from taking what I want and getting that satisfaction. It's good for me to have whatever I want, it's good for my health, my well being, a voice screamed out in Kato's head.

Finch strutted across the room.

"When you feel empowered, you feel great, when you feel great, your energy builds as does your sense of well being. Your life force builds, your health increases. Do you understand that?" Finch cried out. Finch went from the far left of the stage to the far right like Mick Jagger. His flat British accent followed him as he walked.

"You'll get everything you ever wanted. You'll create your life the way you want it." His voice rose as he finished the sentence with an emphatic shake of the head. His bristly mullet shook on top.

Kato got it. He remembered the times when he felt on top of the world, he felt that elation and grandeur in his nerves. He felt charged, and on top of his game. He was soaring.

Finch began giving examples of how morality has kept humans from enjoying themselves.

"Go ahead, indulge yourself in the feeling, the feeling of winning, of victory. These victorious memories will bring you into the present. Recreate that feeling right now in all that you choose. Repeat it again and again and again," he shouted in ecstatic, demonic tones.

Time sped forward. It was suddenly lunch break. Finch looked at his watch.

"We're going to take a break. I want you to know that I am serving you tuna sandwiches on white bread. The meal is catered by St. Abernathy

Church. You paid fifteen thousand dollars to take this seminar and you're going to be fed leftover sandwiches from the church's soup kitchen. It was their Kiddicare lunch from yesterday. The meal includes a lovely tomato soup, and the cost to me is nothing. I want you to know I'm making an enormous amount of money from you. I'm practicing what I'm preaching." Finch smiled and gloated.

"I'm rubbing your faces in it, and that's what I want to do. You see, I'm loving it! Watch me enjoy it! I have no voice in my head saying it's wrong. I'm joyful and fulfilled that I'm getting great sums of money and you're getting leftover soup and sandwiches. I won and I'm so happy about it. I don't owe you anything. You understand? That's how it works. Take advantage. Do what enriches you. Learn from this. Take, take, take! And enjoy the brilliant energy of your uplifted and powerful wellbeing." Finch shouted at them.

"This is life at its best. It is your true self taking flight for the first time. I have the upper hand and I'm taking advantage of you. You understand?!"

Kato's anger rose. He was pissed off. Here was a man with no considerations, no hesitations about making money and filling himself with great satisfaction. He had no moral compunction to provide an amazing meal to his audience just because they paid a lot of money to attend his course. Fuck them!

Finch was free of that kind of thinking. He was entitled to have the health-giving pleasure of fulfilling his desires. He was free of any inhibitions that would prevent him from having the completion of his desires. This was true health.

Finch's words echoed inside Kato.

"Inhibit your gratification, and you undermine your health." It made grand sense to Kato. He ran with it. He imagined himself free, willful and powerful beyond any cultural values and morals. He was like a philosophy student who had just read his first Nietsche essay and was sailing into the blue sky on the permission given to take the reins of his own life and ride as hard and as far as he wished.

Kato was spinning his own wheel of fortune, he was fully empowered. He had never felt this way before. This was beyond cocaine. He was euphoric from this great emotional release. Nothing could stop him in his quest for self satisfaction, and gratification. He deserved it and it was his destiny.

I can do this! I don't need a second rate Rod Stewart yelling at me. I can do it better. I'm gonna beat him at his own game. I'm gonna ruin him, and it's gonna feel great. Kato's smug anger tipped the scales. His competitive nature had given him immense confidence and strength.

Kato ate his tuna on white bread and sipped tomato soup at the communal tables. He had built a castle in the air from Finch's solid words.

Kato watched Alec Finch glide about the room, nodding and greeting many of the attendees as they ate. Kato noticed Finch's hairdo up close. The dry and repulsive attempt to portray himself as a jaunty man-about-town, successful, and in tune with the times, was an empty theatrical parody of success.

Finch was trying too hard. He wasn't successful, he couldn't be, thought Kato. He's no bon vivant. He's an ex-professor or something, used to filling people's heads with nonsense. A hip, learnèd intellectual who had figured out a way to present a strategy. Finch wasn't free. He was a gifted lecturer, a fake who presented ideas, not a transformed man at all.

As he rounded the nearest table, Kato could see the shine of skincare products on his face: a combination of stage makeup and spray tan. Kato watched the sweat coming from Finch's temple slide down the side of his cheek carrying the tan coating like scum on top of a pond. It landed on his white shirt collar.

As he approached, Kato spoke out. His anger, and arrogant spite formed his words.

"If you're so successful, what's with that awful haircut?!" Kato yelled in a loud intimidating voice.

Alec flinched as if he had never been insulted before. He was visibly shaken. No more Mr. Cool, on top of his game, taking life in his stride. The words struck him to the core. Kato saw this moment of weakness and pounced.

"I thought so. Tongue tied when real life gives you a kick in the nuts, Eh?"

Alec smiled, imitating geniality, and spoke.

"Well, heh heh, you might have caught me just a little off guard," he chuckled.

Alec turned and walked towards his dressing room. The shocked and disturbed expression on his face could not be seen by the attendees. All their turned heads could see was his back as he left the room.

Kato addressed the retreating Finch.

"You asked us at the beginning, to tell you our wildest desire? Well, I never told you my wildest desire. So here it is, Finch."

Finch turned.

Kato looked around the room at the astonished group. He had everyone's attention.

"My wildest desire is to do what you're doing here today, Finch. Yes, but I'm going to do it better, and more than that, I'm gonna drive you out of business in this town. I'll send you and your pathetic, sorry ass mullet packing back to merry old England."

Kato turned and left the building.

Chapter 6

Kato pulled out all the stops to make his own seminar happen. He called it GRAB training. The workshop to end all workshops. One that would put an end to Alec Finch's exhortations to the human spirit.

In contrast, Kato created a posh super star event in the Ritz Carlton Hollywood ballroom, chandeliers, fragrant oils, subtle lighting, theater seating, carrera marble walls, walnut woodwork trim. Kato called in favors he didn't know he had, to make it happen. His Uncle Phil's name held sway and everyone was on board.

For $15K, every Hollywood somebody was there with a date, paid in full. The lemon and pomegranate water on the sideboards were decorated with flowers to uplift the spirit. It was nearly a full house of 600 people. Enough to blow Alec Finch out of the workshop game entirely.

The lights dimmed, the spotlight came on. Applause. Kato walked to the microphone. Tall and handsome, Kato nodded in acknowledgement.

"Thank you for being here tonight."

"I'll start with a question: Are you completely here?" He looked around the room.

"I say you're not completely here. I say you've forgotten part of yourself. You've left that part home."

"We are surrounded by abundance and yet we make do with what we earn. How about that? Acting like you're satisfied."

Kato began to work himself into a rhythm. He stepped in cadence and his toned trim form demonstrated to the audience the body language that represented success, domination, control.

"What did you leave at home? Everyone wants to know." The group chuckled.

"You forgot that part of you that wants everything, whenever and whatever it might be!" Kato paced. A silent metronome beat behind his speech.

"You're all rich. I know that. You wouldn't be here unless you knew you were missing out on something. Let me tell you folks. You are. You're missing out on taking all you want." His pacing continued.

"You're all living under the preposterous delusion that you don't choose to get everything you want, because you have a conscience. That you're holding back because you think it's not right! That it would be greedy to have it all, to get all you want as much as you want!" Kato loosened his bow tie and opened his shirt.

"Let me tell you. The old program that your parents implanted, that was handed down for generations, is what makes you sick." He wiped sweat off his brow and strutted like a surly rooster.

"You need to BRAG about it. Be proud of it. Announce it to the world. You think you have to repent because you're rich? Nonsense."

"Let me tell you. All the money you paid for this seminar? I'm keeping it all. All the money goes to me. And I'm up here telling you, you need to gloat." Kato nodded toward the wings and a stage hand came out to take his tux jacket. GRAB practice was broken into parts: how to create a surprise attack; How to maintain the Grab; How to go through the struggle and come out on top. Each part had an exercise that would lead to great success.

"When you gloat, every inflammatory response in your body decreases. **G**et **R**ich **a**nd **B**rag. G-R-A-B. GRAB! Take it. Own it. The pride you feel has healing power. I'm making so much money from this one seminar, it's amazing. $22.5 million for one weekend and I love it! Give me a round of applause." The audience applauded. Kato points to the first row.

"You sir, with the check shirt. C'mon up." The man stood and trotted up the steps to the stage. Kato looked at the man's name tag and retreated to a table behind him. He returned with a rubber doll.

"Don, reach out and take this doll." The man put his hand round the middle of the doll. He pulled, Kato pulled back harder, the man pulled back himself, and wrenched it out of Kato's hand.

"How did that feel, Don? Did you like the thrill of dominance? You took it by force out of my hand." Kato turned to the audience.

"C'mon people you gotta feel the thrill. GRAB it! GRAB IT HARD. IT'S YOURS. OWN IT." Kato's voice rose evangelically.

"You can have anything you want. I want you all to get that feeling." He nodded to the backstage assistant and six support people ran immediately into the audience and passed out rubber dolls. Soon half the group held a doll.

"Turn to your neighbor and take that fucking doll out of their hands. Don't let them have it. Do it! Do it now!" He yelled.

The audience became excited and the greed started to build. Outbursts were occurring all across the room. There was a small shoving match that was quickly stopped by an usher.

"Get that doll chump. Take it. Grab it hard. Feel that rush. It's yours, not his or hers, it's yours. All yours. That feeling, that winning feeling rushes through your blood." Kato shouted.

"You feel that? How good is that? Now switch dolls. That's right, give it to your partner and let them GRAB the doll. Do it!. Take it. Own it. Rip it out of their hands. Gloat, brag about it. You've got it and they don't. Do you get that thrill? That's what it's about."

Don was still on stage holding his doll, watching the audience processing the feeling of greed and the powerful satisfaction that filled them. Kato walked over to Don and ripped the doll out of his hands.

"Gimme that! It's mine now. I own it. And you don't" Kato towered over the cowering Don as he pronounced his dominance.

"You're in the groove now people. You've got the doll, now tell your weak partner how much you love having it. You took it from them, now brag to them. You got it. Lord it over them. Gloat. Brag. GRAB it. It's yours. Do it."

The cacophony of voices rose. Their faces twisted with bragging pride and domination. Kato scanned the group. He knew he was getting through to them by their excited sneers. The victorious doll grabbers played take-away. Body language said: "It's mine, it's mine. I win, you lose."

"Now switch. Take the doll away. It's not just a doll, it's what's missing in your life, the power to take, to be the victor, to dominate. You're the strong one, they're weak. Tell them they're losers. Say it."

Kato had the group pass the dolls to the attendants when the exercise ended.

"Now that you know what it feels like to grab, to own, to feel that domination, I want you to stand up and put your hands on your chest. Feel the power you have. Kato paused while they followed his directions.

"Okay sit down. When you leave here, you're gonna practice what you learned, to reinstate your pride in the victory of greed. You assholes are so rich, you don't understand the unique pleasure and the unique nourishment that bragging provides. Have you ever felt the power of dominating someone who has less, someone you have taken advantage of? This is your homework."

Kato began to rant. His voice rose and fell. He pointed emphatically. He deliberately worked past their lunch time to make them more vulnerable.

"I want you to find someone during the day before the next session. Keep your eyes open. Identify their weakness. Are they gullible? Do they feel inferior? Are they depressed? Alienated? Sad?" Kato changed his posture to act out each described deficit as he said it.

"Is the person impoverished? That's way easier. Once you have a handle on their weakness, take advantage. They may have nothing you want. You need to practice identifying your mark. You need to practice maintaining your grab. You need to practice bragging." He noticed a woman in the audience in a pink dress.

"You, in Pink," Kato shouted and pointed. The woman pointed to herself as if to say, "Me?"

"Yeah, you. You need this work. You grew up with money. You don't know fuck all about working a day in your life."

Kato motioned backstage and out came a poorly dressed man. He walked down into the audience and stood in a slouch beside her.

"I want you to slap him! That's right. Slap his face." Surprised, she gave a small gentle slap to his face.

"No. I want to see dominance. You hear me? Where the fuck have you been? On your cell phone?" Kato screamed.

"Hit him. Curse at him. Yell into his face. Say: I'm rich and you're not. Tell him!" The pink lady blushed as she said the phrases without any emotion.

"No, no, no, you hear that folks? You hear that whiny little rich girl voice. That weak empty voice. She's ready to eat shit." Kato ran into the audience with the microphone.

"You ready to eat shit missy? You have no idea of the power you have. You sit there smug and pretty, everything you wanted was given to you." At this point Kato turned to the group and gesticulated while berating her.

"You never had that desire, that drive, that urge because you were spoiled. She's spoiled, ladies and gentlemen. She never had to fend for herself. She has never felt her own urges. Look at her." Kato stepped back and waved his hand.

"All dressed up nice and pretty. Like a doll, like Barbie. Never had an urge in her life. No anger unless Mommy or Daddy said 'No' to her when she wanted a new dress or shoes. She doesn't know how to want, or how to grab for whatever she wants." Kato worked the crowd into a frenzy with his swelling soliloquy.

"She's like a mealy watermelon, soft and mushy inside, not really sweet. When you taste it, it's unpleasant. You don't want any part of it. You get that sister? You need the greed! Need the greed." Kato turned to address the audience.

"When you go home, I want you to access that part of you that loves the feeling you had here today. That part of you that is nourished by the power, the victory, the dominance, those feel-good healthy emotions that have been shunned and bred out. Get Healthy. BRAG!"

Kato continued to lambast Pink Lady.

"Here she stands, an example of someone who is missing a vital part of her soul. Slapping this guy is not the answer. It's just a demonstration that she is disconnected from her power. Don't go slapping people. There are far easier ways to dominate. Okay. That's it for now. You have twenty minutes for lunch. Let's all give ourselves a round of applause. It's been a helluva morning. Thank you all."

While the crowd roared with applause, Kato stepped forward and shook the pink lady's hand. She smiled sheepishly and told him how deeply grateful she was for making her aware of her issues.

After lunch, Kato reviewed the GRAB premise: Get Rich And Brag. He continued using numerous exercises to train the group through each part of the GRAB process of taking and loving it. At the end, he was worn out.

"Reach out, grab the air before you..." Kato was relentless. He demanded and demeaned, insulted, exhorted, and encouraged. The group worked hard and Kato was a tough taskmaster".

Kato waited for the room to be completely quiet before he spoke again.

"Before you end your day, follow up on your mark. Remember that you own them. Do not let up on them. Tomorrow, our final day together is about domination." He looked around the still room.

"By the end of day tomorrow you will have regained that part of you that has been missing. The part of you that acts from its original nature. You will be back to wholeness. You will have your natural urges intact again, healthy, unrepressed, fully functional. 'The deep joy of gratified desire' will be yours. See you at 9. Don't be late."

As Kato walked off the stage he was met by an assistant

"Look at this," the assistant held a news article in his face. It read: GRAB seminar, a multi-million dollar success. Kato took the paper home with him. He read the short article repeatedly with increasing pride. He had done it. He had made his mark.

Chapter 7

Kato was up by 6 am to do his usual morning workout and smoothie regimen. It was his last day of the seminar. The shower was his magic place to work through his talking points for the day. Domination was the topic. He allowed the water to beat down on him as he ran through the day.

By the end of the shower he was in the zone. He had created a vision for the last day of the training. He had choreographed the entire program, what he would cover and how to proceed. Nothing was written down; it was all in his head.

He stayed focused on his message as he drank his smoothie. He continued forward in a meditative state. Nothing mattered but what he wanted to deliver. He put on simple clothes, nothing formal. He needed to be able to move with agility. He wanted no encumbrances. When he walked to the front door, his car was waiting to take him. When he arrived, his assistants had been there for two hours making sure everything was spotlessly perfect.

As the crowd filtered in and sat, Kato looked about the room and began speaking.

"Domination is the ability to completely control any opposition and to maintain control absolutely during your engagement. Remember your satisfaction comes from your gratified desire. It comes from your taking what you want and bragging about your accomplishment. Sneering in the face of an adversary and gloating about your victory is part of the satisfaction."

As he spoke, Kato noticed someone come in late and sit in the back. Something about the man's gait triggered his attention. While he continued speaking, he looked at the man. It was clear to Kato that the man was wearing a wig and a false mustache. There was no mistake. The wig was at an angle that indicated it was hastily put on. The mustache, a large brushy affair, was too big for his face and the large eyeglasses were peculiar as well. Alarms went off in Kato's head.

As he walked toward the man, Kato continued to lecture.

"Once you have him in your grasp you must hold him firmly." The groups' heads turned as they followed Kato toward the last row. Kato noticed the pointed black shoes and the final alarm bell rang. Kato continued to speak and in one quick motion pulled the wig off the disguised man in the end seat in the last row. The rock star mullet burst forth. It was Alec Finch!

The audience watched raptly and let out a surprised "UH!" Kato set his mic down and grabbed Finch by the collar and pulled him up to standing. Finch was startled, but his eyes blazed with ferocious anger. He struggled to get free, but the stronger Kato held him firmly. Finch must have thought he would never be recognized amid a garish Hollywood throng.

Dragging Finch towards the door, Kato said, "Get out. Now!" in a seething angry voice, quiet enough for only Finch to hear. Finch looked around, then stopped struggling. He glared furiously at Kato, as Kato frog-marched him out. Finch's hands, spastic in front of his chest, fingers fiddling like a cartoon mouse, pulled to his toes by Kato's powerful grip, could do nothing else except submit as he was dragged out the door.

Once outside the banquet room doors, Kato leveled his gaze and spoke with deadly conviction, "If I ever see your face again, no one else ever will. I own you. You are finished." Kato released Finch with a shove. The wigless, mullet-haired Alec Finch looked around briefly, and hurried out through the lobby.

With the charm and aplomb of a professional actor, Kato donned the demeanor of one who had just been inconvenienced by a momentary interruption and began to speak again.

"Domination creates the certainty that your control is never interrupted. I want you to face the person next to you and grab his collar. Draw him or her to you and say: "I own you.""

The group followed his directions. Each successive exercise embodied Kato's own anger at Finch. Kato felt the shock of Finch's intrusion continue throughout the day. It didn't stop him from teaching well, though it did influence his tone as the day progressed. His indignation grew as he brooded. He would become momentarily distracted while he instructed and directed and trained the group and at every pause, his resentment returned.

"Thank you for coming and for being part of this amazing seminar. We will be having subsequent classes and you will be notified."

The mood in the room was jubilant. The empowered attendees were standing tall and looking around to see who they could take advantage of. Their new found predatory joy had grown into an engaging lifestyle instantly. They were ready to go and seize the day, and GRAB all they could.

"Thank you for making this an enormous success. If you want to practice some of the techniques and review how you regained your lost life force, there will be classes coming up. Thank you all for being here. Please GRAB your gift bag on the way out." Kato waved to them all and remained onstage as they left. His thoughts immediately went to Finch. A mixture of fear and rage filled him. He hated to admit it to himself, but the encounter had rattled him.

"That little pipsqueak," he muttered as he turned to leave.

Chapter 8

At home that night, Kato didn't enjoy the triumph of a successful seminar. He just couldn't stop replaying his ugly confrontation with Alec Finch. It really threw him off his stride in the seminar. He couldn't stop seeing in his mind's eye the defiant, rage-filled look on Finch's face. Finch had such a determined look of anger and humiliation. It was a look that told Kato everything he needed to know: Finch would never give up harassing him. Sitting there, replaying the encounter, Kato came to a realization: Finch would have to be dealt with, once and for all.

The next morning, when Kato woke up, he had a plan. It was going to be dicey and outrageous. There was a possibility of exposure. As he sat in bed, he knew that once he took this fateful step, there would be no going back. He thought over the risks. He knew that no careful person, like Uncle Phil, would ever go down this path. But Kato's inner devil, the gambler and addictive risk taker shouted in his ear: *Do it, do it, do it.*

As he picked up the telephone, full of revenge and anger, he thought of his Father, a man he had never known, and who he had the greatest contempt for. Kato's deceased Mother Celine met Leo Worsen, a professional basketball player from Germany, when she was an art student in Berlin in the late 90's. They had a torrid affair, followed by pregnancy, a quick marriage, followed by non-stop arguments, and finally a quick divorce, all in the span of months. When things got real, Leo wanted out, and Celine was glad to see him go. She moved back to Los Angeles.

During Kato's childhood, she spoke very little about Leo, except to say 'he was the most beautiful man I ever met, not including you Kato darling.' Kato never heard from Leo. At age 10, after his mother died, Kato reached out to his Father several times, by mail, and email, but Leo never responded. *Why? He always asked himself. It's not fair. What have I done wrong?* All through his adolescence, his Father's abandonment was the deepest pain. It took Kato to dark places. And here he was again.

With the phone in his hand, still undialed, the rage Kato now felt towards Finch reminded him of his childhood anger towards Leo Worsen. It was such a familiar feeling. Kato knew that this dark well trod path never took him anyplace good. It led deeper and deeper into the darkness. A small part of him didn't want to go.

Do it, do it, do it, said the devil on his shoulder. He called Lisa at the studio.

"Hi Lisa, it's Kato. How are you?"

"Busy as usual." Kato heard sounds of equipment and voices in the background. She muffled the phone and shouted to someone.

"What do you need, Kato?" She sounded wary.

"I need a telephone number."

"Who?"

"Danika Wrin?"

"What? Danika Wrin? What do you want with that snake?"

"It's personal."

"Yeah, ok, well let me tell you something *personal* in return. Whatever it is you have on your mind with her, don't do it. You don't want to have anything to do with her. Trust me. She is bad news."

"Do you have her number or not?"

"If I had her number, I wouldn't give it to you." She hung up.

It took Kato a few more phone calls to a few more contacts, some of whom gave him the same advice, until he had Danika Wrin's personal cell phone number.

He sat on the couch and breathed deeply. He was at a crossroads. Once he made this call, things were going to get nasty for Finch. Things were going to get real for Kato, too. Danika Wrin would also know who Kato Worsen was. Did he dare risk that?

Do it, do it, do it.

He called. She picked up after one ring.

"Beverly Hills Searchlight."

"Danika Wrin?"

"Yes. That's me. And my caller ID says you are Kato Worsen. Hmm, Worsen, Worsen. That name rings a bell somewhere."

"I'm calling because I have a story for the Beverly Hills Searchlight. It's a really good scandal story. You're going to love it."

"Ok, Mr. Kato Worsen. Can you meet me at Fiori's off Rodeo Drive, in a couple of hours, say 12 noon? You can tell me why your name sounds familiar to me, and also you can also tell me about your big story. Get a table outside on the sidewalk cafe. Don't be late." She hung up.

Arriving early at 11:30 am, Danika Wrin pulled her BMW convertible up to Fiori's, a super swank gathering place for Hollywood elites and anybody who wanted to be seen by the paparazzi. She unfolded her elegant showgirl legs out of the car, handed her keys to the valet, shook her full head of gorgeous, honey-blond hair, and smiled at seeing her casual clad bodyguards, already sitting two tables from her normal spot, which was directly in front of the security cameras and microphones.

She was tanned and relaxed, having just returned yesterday from three glorious unplugged months away from her LA life, idling on the beaches and bistros of the French Riviera and Sardinia. When Kato called this morning, he was the first potential story source she had talked to since her return. She had no idea what was going on in the seamy side of LA right now. However, she was confident that the dark and dirty news would soon find its way to the Beverly Hills Searchlight. It always did.

Danika, a part owner of Fiori's, had called ahead and set up the "usual": cameras and microphones to record everything said to her, with bodyguards to handle any unpleasantness.

Danika was a very well preserved 49 years old, who looked no older than 40. If you met her on the street, you'd think she was a one time midwest cheerleader, until you looked into her eyes, and saw her sharp, suspicious and shrewd nature. She grew up in an unhappy, ultra-Christian household in Nebraska. At 18, Danika left home forever, seeking a showgirl spot in Las Vegas. With her looks and confidence, she easily got a spot in the chorus line.

She studied journalism at college by day and danced at night. Focused and smart, she graduated in three years, and landed a job with the Las Vegas Tribune. After five years she had her own column, a popular, funny, irreverent salacious gossip and rumor feature called "Whispers on the street." For ten years she built and guarded her column with skill and professionalism by double checking her stories to avoid defamation.

Proudly she had never been sued, despite causing enormous humiliation and ruining countless reputations. Everything was going perfect for her until she ran an embarrassing but true story about beloved Las Vegas icon Wayne Newton. That was too much for the paper. She was fired.

Unfazed, Danika drifted west to Los Angeles where she started her scalding online blog "Beverly Hills Searchlight." She cultivated sources, bought stories, and sold some stories to mainstream papers and Hollywood trade magazines.

Always on the razor's edge of defamation, Danika thrived in LA. She didn't care who she ruined and she loved being her own boss. No timid editors looked over her shoulders, and no guardrails kept her from saying whatever she wanted.

She was hated by everybody with money, prestige or fame in the movie industry. That was an expected byproduct of her stories. The rich and connected were the fish in her pond. She didn't go after ordinary citizens. The higher someone climbed the fame ladder, the more interested she was in bringing out the ugliest gossip about them. Her online circulation grew every year. She was famous and photogenic, and she was having the time of her life.

As she walked onto the patio of Fiori's, she nodded at the waiter, who brought her usual Campari and soda. Pushing her sunglasses up into her thick hair, Danika nodded to her bodyguards, and spoke a few soft words to herself, as the bodyguards adjusted the volume on the directional microphone. She checked her purse to make sure her pepper spray was easily at hand.

Danika was ready. At 11:55 am, Kato Worsen walked onto the patio. He looked around. A stunning woman in a cream colored skirt and off-white blouse saw him looking around. She nodded. Kato walked over.

"I'm Kato Worsen."

"Danika Wrin." They shook hands. She sat and pulled a small laptop from her handbag, opened it and asked: "Is that spelled 'Worsen'?"

"Correct," said Kato. She typed in name name, and looked at the screen for a brief moment. She nodded and looked up at him.

"Ok, Kato. You said you had a story. Spill."

"I'm being harassed by a man named Alec Finch, who has been running a questionable seminar series called Socio-Ortho-Genomics. I want him to leave me alone. He's an awful person."

"Alec, with a 'c' or a 'k'?"

"C."

She looked Alec Finch up on the internet. She scrolled down the screen.

"Ooh. I see. There's a lot here on Mr. Finch."

"That's right. I attended his seminar. He's feeding people stale cookies in a church basement, and charging them $15,000 for his seminar."

"Really?" She looked up Socio Orth-Genomics, and read for a few moments.

"From what I can see, he's teaching a very mean and unorthodox philosophy. It's basically a version of "Greed is Good", right? Tell me more"

Kato told her everything about the class he took. He ended by telling her how sensitive Finch is about his Rod Stewart hair, and about the moment when Alec flinched when Kato asked him: "If you are so successful, why do you have that stupid haircut."

Of course, he failed to mention that Kato had copied Socio-Ortho-Genomics, turning it into his much more profitable GRAB training.

"His hair is like Rod Stewart's?" asked Danika.

"He has a thing for Rod Stewart, a fetish actually."

She looked this fact up.

"Oh, dear. Rod Stewart filed a restraining order in London against Mr. Finch. There are others filed in different US cities. Take a look at this."

She turned the screen towards Kato, showing a very unflattering black and white gotcha tabloid photo. In the picture, Alec Finch was caught in a snarling grimace outside of a London courthouse.

She scrolled through other Alec Finch stories.

"Here is something about his involvement with 'The Rock Star Hair Fan Club.'" She read for a while, then shook her head.

"What a bunch of wackos. Not exactly the type of people we want in our fair city of Los Angeles. No wonder he emigrated." She shut her laptop.

"Ok. The story basically writes itself. No research necessary. All the facts are on the internet. You want him smeared? Then it's $10,000 for me to write a hatchet job piece on Alec Finch."

"$10,000? Are you kidding? You want $10,000? Aren't you a journalist? Don't you just report the news?"

She sniffed, and looked at Kato with those ice cold blue eyes.

"Here are your choices, Mr. Worsen. You can either pay me $10,000 in the next half hour, and I write a humiliating piece that will ruin Finch, or I will take this same story to Finch this afternoon and offer to kill the story forever for $20,000. Believe me: he will pay. One thing you should know is that when I kill a story, it stays dead. No journalist or blogger in this town will ever take up your story against Finch after I have killed it. They all know better, because I know where all the bodies are buried, figuratively and literally. Those are your options."

Kato sat back. He was stunned. He had no choice, "I'll pay."

"Good boy."

Kato opened up his phone to access his bank account. In a few minutes the money was transferred.

"Have a good day, Kato Worsen."

He left, with mixed feelings. On the one hand, given Danika Wrin's well-known and well-established track record of ruining people in Hollywood,

Finch was definitely going down, and going down hard. He wouldn't recover. Kato, the aggressive GRAB trainer part of him, felt glad.

On the other hand, he recalled Lisa's warning about avoiding Danika Wrin at all costs. Having just met her, Kato couldn't deny that Lisa was correct. Danika was one of the most dangerous gossip columnists anywhere, a woman without scruples, conscience or compassion. She couldn't be controlled. As he walked away, he was having second thoughts about his angry plan to ruin Finch.

Chapter 9

Two days later, Alec Finch was stuck in morning rush hour traffic on the I-405 freeway when his phone rang. The caller ID said the single word "searchlight". Having nothing better to do while waiting for traffic to unsnarl, he answered.

"Alec Finch?" asked the woman caller.

"Yes."

"This is Danika Wrin of the Beverly Hills Searchlight. Would you care to comment on the story about you that was just released on our website. If you have a comment after reading the story, respond in the next hour and I can include your response on the website, and also in the same story that will be released this afternoon in the Los Angeles Times, the San Francisco Chronicle, and in Variety magazine."

"Whhhhat?"

"Is that your comment? Can I quote you?"

"What story about me? I don't know of any story."

"Of course not. It just came out a few minutes ago. Are you connected to the internet?"

"I'm in my car, but I think so."

"Good. Go to the Beverly Hills Searchlight website and read the story. Comment if you would like to be quoted."

"What?"

"Good bye." Danika Wrin hung up.

Alec Finch found the Beverly Hills Searchlight website and then the story, which was the top feature on the website. The story was titled: "Alec Flinched, a series of unfortunate flinches." Above the story was that old paparazzi photo of him grimacing on the courthouse steps, after Rod Stewart obtained his restraining order.

Oh no.

He read the story, and felt like he was punched in the gut. The writer, who identified herself as Danika Wrin, found every embarrassing detail of his life, and displayed them in the most humiliating way for the world to see and laugh at him. The mean and predatory Socio Ortho-Genomics was a main theme, but his other failures, as a bass player and as a drummer were also there.

There was a sidebar on the 'Rock Star Hair Fan Club.' The sidebar showed photos of only the gnarliest, mullet-wearing members in the club.

The exposure lit a fire of humiliation and shame in Alec. He was no longer a member of a mostly unknown eccentric club, flying under the radar in LA. He was now forever exposed for public ridicule. Danika Wrin was truly an expert at finding a person's weak spot.

Anyone reading the story would think Alec was a complete fool, and a dishonest leech sucking money out of society. He knew he had nothing to say as a comment, because it was all the truth.

I'm ruined. Nobody will come to Socio Ortho-Genomics after this story. I'm a laughingstock. It's all over. Traffic started up. Alec was numb as he drove home.

Who could have done this to me? Finch had been hosting seminars for a couple of months without any adverse publicity.
But as he drove he recalled Kato Worsen's threat on the day Kato threw him out of GRAB training: 'I own you. You are finished.'

He remembered the furious look on Kato's face. *This is Kato's fault. I'm sure of it.*

Chapter 10

Alec Finch was so distracted and angry while driving home he almost ran a red light. At another stop light, he nearly plowed into the car in front of him. But he made it. Inside his house he paced around fuming and fretting. Socio Ortho-Genomics was finished, and he knew he would always be nothing but a laughingstock in LA. In his mind everyone was pointing and snickering at him. How could he show his face anywhere after this?

As he paced around his house, he instinctively knew that he had to do something to distract himself. But what? Then it came to him. His anger at Kato showed him the way. *I'll ruin Kato.*

He went to his computer and googled Kato Worsen. He found very little. Kato had existed largely under the social radar. He found out that Kato was related to Phil Giardia, the head of a major studio. There was little else. *There must be more. Maybe Kato has been sued.*

He would have to go to the Los Angeles County Courthouse to check public records, on the off chance he could find something to use against Kato. He immediately got back in his car, this time he drove carefully.

At the County courthouse, he found a public information terminal and plugged in Kato's name. Up popped a long list of lawsuits against Kato, stretching back years. Most were people and businesses suing Kato for bad debts. Kato never paid anyone.

As he scanned the list, one lawsuit popped out. It was different. It was a lawsuit for assault and sexual battery filed by a woman named Michelle Weeks. The case had been dismissed shortly after it was filed. *Assault and sexual battery civil charges against Kato brought by a woman. This is hopeful. It appears Kato was a bad boy.*

He looked up the case, and found the woman's name and address and phone number. Sitting at the computer terminal, he called Michelle Weeks. She answered on the first ring.

"Michelle Weeks?"

"Yes."

"My name is Alec Finch. I read about the lawsuit you brought a few months ago against Kato Worsen. He has also caused me harm. Can I ask you a couple of quick questions about your lawsuit?"

There was a long pause, then Michelle spoke.

"Yeah. I'm sorry. I withdrew that lawsuit after talking to my lawyer."

To Finch, she sounded like she was just a teenager.

"But Kato hit you, right? He tried to rape you? You sued him for assault and sexual battery."

She paused for a long time.

"No. Actually, he just owed me money." She paused. "He owed me for – you know – something I couldn't legally sue him for. My lawyer told me to drop it."

Finch's heart sank. Her vagueness told him that she had been trying to collect for a drug deal. There was no assault and no sexual battery. He was about to thank her and hang up, when she said, "Kato is a first class asshole. After I dismissed the lawsuit I heard he did something really bad up in Oregon. It's unbelievable, but it's true."

Finch sucked in a big breath. "What happened in Oregon?"

"I know these guys so I bet on it being true. I've known these two since high school, Carlo Berkino and Jonah Wilsky. They don't know Kato. This past summer they were up in Montana working for a guy who was once a bigshot LA realtor named Brent Gardner. They were up there learning to be cowboys or something."

"Okay. What happened?"

"They told me that Brent Gardner was part of a screenwriting team working in the middle of nowhere in Oregon. Brent had an idea for a movie based on true events. He sold the story to a studio, and was part of the screenwriting team. The studio told the screenwriters they had to write the screenplay fast."

"Okay."

"So Carlo and Jonah said, Brent Gardner went to Oregon, but returned to Montana two days later, mad as hell at Kato. Brent told everyone this crazy story about Kato going on a rampage. The screenwriters barely escaped with their lives."

Finch was now very interested.

"Really?"

"Yeah. According to my friends, who heard it from Brent Gardner, Kato was supposed to just be the cook during this writer's retreat. But instead he was snorting cocaine non-stop and went insane. He got some guns. and kidnapped the screenwriters. Kato threatened to kill them all. And he was going to torture them before he killed them."

"Did you say torture, Michelle?"

"Yeah. Kato tied up the three screenwriters. He told them he was going to put them outside in dog cages with cactus and fire ants and porcupines.

He was going to make them eat out of dog bowls, and howl and bark instead of talking. He was gonna make them run naked into the desert and hunt them for sport. He was going to put rattlesnakes and wild ferrets in the cages too."

"Wow. That's awful."

"Oh yeah. It sounds unbelievable, but I can tell you that Kato's a jerk."

"I know that. How did the screenwriters escape?"

"According to Brent, Kato went out for just a few minutes. Brent Gardner had a hidden knife in his boot. He freed himself and the others, and he stood guard until the others escaped. Brent said he yelled out to Kato to come out and fight him, but Kato ran away."

"Wow."

"Yeah, but the part about Kato running away scared doesn't sound like Kato. Uh uh. No. He's an ass, but he's a crazy daredevil. I can't see him backing away from danger. I once saw him bungee jump off a bridge, one that had never been jumped off before. He did it on a dare, totally reckless."

"Huh. Did Brent call the police?"

"I don't think they called the police. Brent just went home to Montana. Brent didn't want to embarrass the studio. He convinced the studio to just sweep it all under the rug, since the screenwriters all escaped with their lives. You need to know that Kato is related to the studio owner. So the studio was glad to agree to Brent's plan. They thanked him for it. Brent told the story to everybody. How heroic he is! But after a while he stopped talking about it entirely for some reason."

"So Carlo and Jonah both heard this story? Do you think I could talk to both of them?"

"Sure. They've been telling people this story for weeks." She gave Finch their telephone numbers.

"Thank you Michelle. I hate Kato more than anybody. Thank you." Finch hung up. He was elated. This was an unbelievable story. Kato might even get arrested and thrown in prison for years for kidnapping and torture. *I'm going to ruin you Kato*, thought Finch. *Yes I am.*

An idea came to him. *Danika Wrin. I have her telephone number now. I'll call her and give Kato a taste of his own medicine.* He called Danika Wrin. She answered on the first ring.

Chapter 11

The next day Alec Finch parked his car near Fiori's restaurant. As he walked up, two burly men stopped him on the sidewalk.

"We need to frisk you, hold your arms out. Don't move." Finch did as he was told.

After they were sure Finch was unarmed, they followed him to the patio of the restaurant, towards Danika Wrin. They sat at the next table, and turned to face Finch. Danika was wearing a dark pantsuit and looked as effortlessly stunning as ever. She had a campari and soda. The waiter didn't come over. Nobody offered Finch a drink. She had her laptop out.

"You are being taped and recorded," she said. "I am here because you told me you have a story for me about Kato Worsen. So tell it, but if you cause any trouble, these men will hurt you, and then you will be arrested. Understand?"

"I understand."

Alec Finch passed Danika a slip of paper with the telephone numbers of Carlo and Jonah, whom Finch had called yesterday, confirming Michelle's outrageous story. Finch told Danika the story about Kato going on a near murderous rampage at Love Dog Ranch in Oregon. She listened impassively.

When he was done, she said.

"I will have to confirm this story via Carlo and Jonah."

"They'll happily talk to you. They told me the story yesterday."

"Okay. You want your revenge against Kato Worsen. I get it. I'm just doing my job. Don't take what I wrote about you personally. I don't know you. I have nothing personal against you."

"It's hard not to take what you wrote personally. You ruined me."

"I understand. Before you get angry at me, remember that I'm very good at what I do. Be grown up about it, okay? If what you tell me pans out, you'll have your revenge."

"Yes."

"Good. Your hit piece against Kato will cost you $10,000, payable in the next half hour. If you don't pay, I'm going to sell Kato the rights to kill the story forever for $20,000. Believe me, he'll pay. If he pays, the story is killed forever. He has the money. I want to do this story, because when Kato asked to meet me, he never disclosed that the two of you were business rivals. He has GRAB training, and you have Socio Ortho-Genomics. You're both swimming in the same pool. I don't like that he failed to disclose that."

"Would knowing that we were rivals have made any difference before you ruined me and my life." Finch's voice rose angrily, and the two bodyguards took immediate notice. They sat on the edge of their chairs. Finch caught the menace, and sat back in his chair.

She thought about this for a moment.

"No. Not really. It wouldn't have made a difference. I'm in business. But I don't like being used. Kato used me, so I now have my own beef with him. So, Alec, I can assure you that if I write and publish a story about Kato Worsen, it is going to hurt him as bad as you got hurt, probably worse. Are you ready to pay?"

He was ready to pay, and in a few minutes, he transferred the funds.

"Pleasure doing business with you, Alec." He left.

Chapter 12

Three days later, while he was preparing for another sold out GRAB seminar scheduled to take place the next day, Kato Worsen received a phone call. The caller ID said Danika Wrin.

"Hello, Kato?"

Kato recognized the voice.

"Yes, Danika. How are you? What can I do for you?"

"Would you care to comment on the story on the website for the Beverly Hills Searchlight that is coming out in the Los Angeles Times tomorrow?"

"I thought I already told you everything I knew about Finch. It was a good story. Why would I need to comment?"

"This story isn't about Finch. This one is about you."

"Me? How dare you! I paid you to write about Finch. What is this?"

"Yes, you paid me to write about Finch, and I did. A few days ago Finch paid me to write about you. That's the story you can comment on if you get back to me in the next half hour. Don't take it personally. It's just business."

"You wrote about me! I thought we had a deal? How much is it going to cost me to kill this story? I'll pay. You should have come to me first. You can't do this. It's unethical."

"That's not how I work. You did him in, and now he's doing you in. And you never told me up front that you were business rivals. You used me, and I don't like that one bit. Read the story. Comment – or not. Goodbye." She hung up.

Numb and fearful, Kato went to the website. He was shocked. He never considered blowback as a possibility, yet here it was. Then he saw the headline. There was a picture of him and Uncle Phil at Phil's last party, both of them in tuxedos, smiling for the cameras. He had to sit down. He felt lightheaded as he read the headline.

"CAIN ENABLED. PAMPERED SHOW BIZ BRAT KATO WORSEN 'GRABS' EVERYTHING HE CAN, LEAVING RUINED LIVES, BAD DEBTS AND TERRORIZED VICTIMS IN HIS WAKE. Former "nice guy" studio Exec Phil Giardia is exposed as the person responsible for years of sheltering and covering up for his infamous predator nephew. Greed, violence, addiction and excess characterizes a wasted life that continually failed...."

Kato looked away from the screen. *She is blaming Uncle Phil for me. Oh no.*

Kato read the entire piece. It was long. It was thorough. At least a dozen people went on the record gleefully documenting true stories of Kato lying, Kato cheating, Kato taking all manner of drugs, Kato screwing over friends, and Kato crashing other people's cars.

Several disgruntled clients from the GRAB training described trying to obtain refunds and being threatened with lawsuits by Kato's lawyers. There were devastating second hand descriptions about Kato threatening to torture and then kill the three screenwriters at the Love Dog Ranch. All three screenwriters declined to comment on the story, but there were plenty of other people who went on record saying: 'Yeah, that sounds just like Kato."

The second half of the story painstakingly pointed out how Phil always paid off or covered up his nephew Kato's abuses, ever since Kato was a teenager.

"I'm ruined. Phil is finished with me."

In a daze, he wandered around his apartment. After a while, he realized he needed distraction. He desperately needed someone to affirm that he was worthy. He got in his Mercedes SUV and started driving. He was thinking of maybe going to a movie. Then he passed a Bentley luxury car dealership. That will do, he thought. I sure don't want a Bentley, but I can let a car dealer try to impress me. He stopped and walked in.

Chapter 13

When Kato got Irv's call he was still at the Bentley dealership pretending he was interested. He was sitting in a driver's seat in the vast showroom.

Kato looked at the caller ID. *It's Irv,* he thought. *Hopefully he hasn't seen the story.*

"Oh hi Irv, just looking at a new car. I'm liking the new Bentley coupe. Have you seen the new one's? They're..."

Irv interrupted him.

"Phil's dying."

"He's been dying for years now, Irv. We know that. Been through all that drama. I have to..."

Irv interrupted again.

"Kato. Stop what you're doing. He's really dying, now. He won't be around long. I'm thinking maybe an hour at most. He's asking for you. Show up, damn it!"

"Okay."

"One more thing, Kato. This morning Danika Wrin called me for a comment on her character assassination story about you. You goddamned son of a bitch. You ruined Phil! Are you happy about that? Damn you." Irv hung up.

Kato gulped.

For a moment, he sat in the big car and felt the leather seats and smelled their aroma. He was surrounded by the shrouded silence of the beautiful car. It kept out extraneous noise and in that moment he was alone with himself. After years of denying his attachment and love for his uncle Phil, he felt something move within. It was an opening that he had guarded and kept closed most of his life.

Since his father had never been there, and his mother died when he was young, that blocked door in his soul was stuffed with pretentious behavior he had invented to prevent feeling the painful moments of devastating loss. It was something he couldn't look at, couldn't allow himself to feel. At that moment, there was a frightful knock at that inner door, and his mood shifted.

Kato got out of the Bentley, walked past the waving salesman who wanted to close the deal, out onto the busy street and into his car. He was wrapped in a dream. No noise on the street phased him. It was as if he was still inside the Bentley with his solitude and his breathing. He felt exposed. There was no hiding.

Kato drove without thinking. Entranced, he entered the tidal river of his pulse and his breath deepend. In what seemed like minutes, he ascended the drive to Phil's estate and was in Phil's bedroom in seconds.

Lisa sat beside Phil and held his hand. Her mascara was smeared and her eyes were teary red. She frowned at Kato. Irv paced the room anxiously, looking out each window he passed. When he saw Kato, he shook his head and gave Kato a look of pure disgust.

Kato kneeled beside the bed. He could see the tufts of dyed black hair that had been allowed to turn to soft gray in the last weeks. It was the hair he had known when he was a kid. In a flood of memories, Kato remembered smelling his uncle's hair when he picked him up and hugged him as a child. He felt a lump in his throat and his tears welled up and overflowed.

Kato leaned in and smelled Phil's hair. His arms went around the dying man. Kato laid his face on Phil's chest and cried deeply. All the years of choked emotion leaped out. He cried and sobbed until he couldn't any longer. Phil's pajama top was soaked. Phil's weak hand had dropped on the back of Kato's head as he cried.

"I love you uncle Phil. I always loved you and I always will. You saved me from a terrible life. I'm so sorry that I acted badly all this time."

Irv came over. He pulled Kato away. He whispered in Kato's ear.

"He hasn't seen the story. Don't tell him. At least spare him that indignity. Could you do that?"

Kato's crying was triggered again. He went back to Phil. He pulled Phil's hand to his forehead and cried again. Lisa and Irv watched quietly, their compassion for Kato worn thin. Kato opened up for the first time in his adult life, before their eyes. His typical hip, smug verve was gone. Before them stood a shambling young man, touched and reduced to his simplest self. He was once more that crying child Phil rescued from trauma and took for his own.

Irv sneered at Kato and shook his head.

Kato held Phil's hand and sobbed. At that moment Phil turned his head toward Kato and let out a soft breath. It was his last. Kato turned and saw Phil's eyes shut.

"Uncle Phil, uncle Phil...no, no, not yet...Oh uncle Phil...not yet." Kato put his head down on his uncle's warm body and shook his head.

Irv was about to reach out and embrace Kato, but he held back and hugged Lisa instead. So many years of Kato's bad behavior had come between Irv and Kato, destroying their once close relationship when Kato was a child. At this moment, Irv hated Kato more than he hated anyone. So many arguments and broken agreements had occurred over the years. Now that a suddenly authentic Kato seemed to emerge at the loss of Phil, Irv felt no desire to forgive Kato and embrace him, comfort him. Kato was a mess. It looked like he might stay next to Phil, blubbering for hours.

"Come on." Irv went to Kato and put his hand on Kato's back. Lisa came near and the two lifted Kato up from his knees and walked him to a chair. Kato stared out the window stunned. Lisa poured water and handed it to Kato.

"I've gotta make it right, Irv. I've had enough. I'm gonna miss the big guy. He saved me and I never showed him the love." Kato sobbed.

"Way too little, years too late."

Lisa looked at Kato and said, "I told you not to go to Danika Wrin, Kato. Remember?"

"What?" Irv spat out the word angrily. "Kato is the one who went to Danika Wrin?" Irv's eyes rose to the top of his head, startled.

"Yeah, Irv," Lisa continued. "Kato financed and pushed the hit piece whose purpose was to take down that weirdo in the mullet, Alec Finch. You know, the guy that was Kato's business rival? The guy who gave you the brochure?"

This was news to Irv and he sat down heavily on a chair.

"Let me get this straight, Kato. Lisa warned you off Danika and you ignored her? That means you started this whole thing. You brought this on. Damn. You ruined Phil's reputation. I couldn't care less if you get ruined, but you, you, you...ruined my best friend and took him down with you. You ruined the best person in the whole fucking movie industry. Now his reputation is trashed forever. In the public mind, Phil will be forever the bad guy who made you into the monster you are. You fucking ruin everything!"

Kato broke down crying. His face in his hands.

"Here's something else to think about, Kato. I'm going to make it my life's work to repair the damage to my dearest friend's good name. I'm going to do it by telling everyone, publicly and privately, that Phil only had one flaw and one character defect, and that was his soft spot for you. His only defect was propping you up all these years. I'm going to tell everyone that you're every bit the worthless person that article makes you out to be. Phil should have tossed you on the street years ago. Now you've ruined him. Thank God, at least he didn't live to read that story. You ruined his life's work. You are terrible."

"I'm so sorry."

Irv snorted in derision.

"Sorry doesn't cut it. You might want to skip the funeral, because I'm giving the eulogy and I'm going to trash you in public, and in the press, to begin the long process of saving Phil's name. Phil's rehabilitation – and your banishment – begins today."

Kato started crying again. "I'm sorry."

"Save it. It's not me you need to apologize to. You should apologize to a few of your other numerous victims. How about doing that for once in your life?"

Kato left, dazed and crying. Outside the mansion, Lisa caught up with him. She was waving a piece of paper in her hand.

"Wait, Kato." He turned.

"You should come to the funeral. Just keep a low profile. I'll make sure Irv doesn't trash you in the eulogy. But, everybody will be talking about the story, myself included, and nobody will have anything good to say about you. Why didn't you listen to me about Danika?"

"I screwed up."

She handed him the piece of paper.

"This is the contact information for the Tropospherence Healing Center outside Ojai. Their healing methods are radical and controversial to say the least. But it's genuine healing. It's not predatory and mean like your GRAB training." She stood back and shook her head in dismay. "What the hell were you thinking, Kato?"

"I've got nothing to say in my defense."

"Tropospherence is located on a couple hundred acres that once was a Christian summer camp. It's very expensive and very exclusive. Privacy is their number one concern. Everyone signs a non-disclosure agreement. They only do one type of program, a 40 day healing retreat, three times a year, with no cell phones, no news, no contact with the outside world. If you leave the Tropospherence Healing Center before the 40 days are over, you can't come back in, and you lose your tuition. They'll sue you if you talk about what goes on there. Check it out. From what I've heard, when a person is disgraced like you, it's the very best and safest place to go when the heat is on. It'll keep you away from bad publicity, and start the process of being forgotten in the public eye."

Kato took the paper, mumbled thanks, and left.

Chapter 14

Back at his house, Kato was exhausted by the morning's activities. In the span of a few hours, he had been ruined by Danika Wrin's story, he had witnessed the death of the only good person left in his life, and he had been banished by Irv. He took a long shower, then slept for 16 hours.

When he woke, he remembered Irv's anger and his advice: You should apologize to your victims.

It made sense. He went to his safe and retrieved Brent Gardner's six shooter, the fancy weapon Richard Boone had used as TV gunfighter Paladin in Have Gun will Travel. He carefully packaged the unloaded gun into a shipping box. Before he closed the box, he included a simple note: 'I'm sorry. Kato.' He called Fedex to pick up the box.

Kato found the phone number for the Evictus Ranch in Montana. He called and identified himself. Brent Gardner's secretary put him on hold. When she came back on the line, she said: "Mr. Gardner does not want to speak to you, ever. If you call again, his lawyers will sue you for harassment." Then she hung up.

I'll try another one.

He called J.J. Pinkus, the sensitive screenwriter from the Love Dog Ranch fiasco, the guy who owned the ferrets.

"J.J. This is Kato Worsen."

A long silence. Then a soft voice said, "What do you want?"

"I'm sorry J.J. I'm awfully sorry. I scared you. I scared everybody. There's no excuse. I hurt you. I was wrong."

Another long silence. Then Kato heard a deep intake of breath.

"Do you know that I couldn't leave my apartment for a month after I got back from Oregon? I was terrified by what you did. Terrified. Do you know that I was in daily contact with my therapist? Do you know that I almost quit the movie business altogether? Do you know that I almost committed myself to a mental institution?" J.J.'s voice rose in volume and anger. He was breathing heavily. "Do you know that?" He screamed.

"No."

"Didn't think so. Fortunately, the studio paid us for the screenwriting job, or I would have been thrown onto the streets. I would have been homeless."

"I'm sorry."

"Well. Things turned around. Irv Gottlieb bought two of my projects and now I'm working again. I have two movies in the works."

"That's excellent. I hope the flying ferretinis are doing ok too. What can I do to help you?"

"Stop. Don't try to be friendly to me. Don't ever contact me again. That's what you can do. I don't like you. I definitely don't trust you. I read the story about you in the Beverly Hills Searchlight. Danika Wrin called me for a comment before it was published. I didn't say a single thing about you. Whatever they heard about the Love Dog Ranch incident, it didn't come from me. That's the truth. You don't have any reason to come after me."

"I know," answered Kato, but J.J. had already hung up.

Chapter 15

Office hours for student questions were almost over for English teacher Walt Journey at Bakersfield Community College. No students had come in today, which was fine. Walt sat back in his chair and surveyed the happy, cluttered mess in his office. There were papers, tests, essays, and books on every surface including the visitor chairs. His office was just the way he liked it. His eyes surveyed the shelf next to his desk, finally settling on a white cowboy hat, with a chunk chewed out of the brim, tossed on top of some papers. It was Brent Garndner's cowboy hat, the hat that once belonged to Roy Rogers.

Walt smiled like he always did. Few colleagues and students who visited his office ever commented on the ruined hat. If anybody ever did mention it, he always said the same thing: "It's the last memento from my days when I was a Hollywood screenwriter." Walt was smiling and looking at his hat when his cell phone rang.

"Walt. This is Kato. Don't hang up. I'm sorry. I'm so sorry."

"Well, hello Kato. What a coincidence. I've been thinking about you recently."

"You mean because of that story about me?"

"Well, no, not just because of the story. That snake Danika Wrin has been striking fear into show biz people for years. How the hell did you ever come onto her radar?"

Kato paused. "Long story short, it was all my fault."

"Wow. You know, I actually believe that. She really put the boots to you. And then she stomped Phil Giardia with you into the dirt. Poor guy. I met him back in the day. I liked him. Everybody did. I heard he died. He was always a good man, someone you could trust, which is rare in the movie business."

"Yeah. He was. I really do want to apologize to you. I need to say I'm sorry. I hurt you. I devastated J.J. He hates my guts. Brent won't take my call. I can't blame him either."

"Well, I'm ok, Kato. Don't worry about it."

"Thanks. That's a relief." Kato paused. "Why were you thinking of me?"

Walt took a deep breath. His eyes looked up at Brent Gardner's cowboy hat. He smiled again.

"Kato, the reason I've been thinking of you is I want to thank you."

"What? *You* want to thank *me*? After what I did?"

"No. Not for what you did. That was totally inexcusable. But I want to thank you, because your near homicidal nonsense stopped me from falling off the wagon. It broke the spell I was under. You didn't know this at the time back at the Ranch, but I was ready to drink again that day, after over 25 years of careful sobriety. The entire screenwriting experience was one huge trigger for me. I really wanted to snort a huge line of your cocaine and get drunk and stay drunk, and work on writing the screenplay, just like I used to do in the old days before I dried out. But if I had taken that drink, or snorted that line, who knows where I would have ended up? The compulsion was so powerful, I was ready to throw my entire life away, but your insane antics stopped me. That's why I want to thank you. I thank God you ruined the screenplay. You saved me."

Kato didn't respond for a long time. He was speechless.

"I didn't expect to hear that. I'm the one trying to make amends."

Walt laughed.

"Crazy isn't it? You call to apologize, and I end up thanking you. That's why I've been thinking of you. In a roundabout way, you saved me, and I'm ever so thankful."

"Sure, anytime." This time they both laughed.

"But wait, Kato, I've got more to tell you."

"More?"

"I need to *apologize* to you, Kato."

"Apologize to me? That's totally nuts."

"Yeah. It is. You know those things Danika wrote about what you were promising to do to us up at Love Dog Ranch, to chain us in the kennels, to make us run naked in the desert while you hunt us, and to torture us with wild animals?"

"Yeah."

"I'm sorry, but I'm responsible for those lies."

"What! You?"

Walt took a deep breath.

"Yeah, me. Here's what happened. You're the first person I've told this to. After you drugged Brent, and he fell asleep, his breathing became shallow and ragged. JJ and I moved him to the couch in front of the fire, and then J.J. fled. He was beyond scared. I was scared too. I wanted to leave with him, but I really thought Brent was going to stop breathing or suffocate on his vomit or something."

"I didn't know that."

"I thought he was going to die. So I stayed. I don't know why. I watched that son of a bitch Brent for hours that night, as he struggled to stay alive. At about 1am, his breathing steadied, and I got a couple hours of sleep. I woke around 4am, to the sound of him packing. He came downstairs. I told him how he almost died. He laughed in my face. He told me I was a nervous nelly. He told me he was never in any danger, that it was all in my head. He gave me no thanks at all. In fact, he wanted me to help him get his gun back from you.Then he tried to get me to drive up to his ranch in Montana so we could finish the screenplay. I refused. By that time, I wanted out of the whole screenplay thing. I was done with everything. He took this refusal personally and started insulting me. He called me a loser and a failure."

"Really?"

"Yeah. I was exhausted, and his insults were too much for me to bear after worrying about saving him. I knew he was scared of you. So I used his fear. I told him that *you* hated *his* guts. I told Brent that *you* were going to make the ferrets gnaw on his genitals. He really got scared when I said that. I improvised. I told him a bunch of other things, some of which you read about. Some of what you read was made up by other people. Anyway, I thought Brent was going to piss his pants."

"Really?"

"I told him you were watching the lodge with the gun, waiting for him to come out the front door, so you could shoot him. He didn't know what to do. He is a bully. I told him that his only hope was to climb out the tiny window in the children's room, then dash quietly around the lodge, get in his truck and drive away fast."

"I didn't know this."

"You are the first person I've told. So anyway, he totally bought my plan. We tossed his gear out the little window. He handed me his cowboy hat to hold. Then he tried to squeeze out the window head first. He is fat so he got stuck. I gave him a huge shove and he flew out the window and landed hard. As soon as he hit the ground, I told him that you had heard him crying out. I told him you were coming for him with the gun. I pretended I couldn't find his hat, and urged him to run for his life. He did."

"Oh my God."

"And I kept the hat."

"You kept his hat? You have Roy Rogers' cowboy hat?"

"Yep. I'm looking at it right now on my shelf."

"Wow."

"But I think it is time for me to give that jerk back his hat."

"No, Walt. Keep the hat. You earned it. That story is priceless. I'll keep your secret."

Walt chuckled.

"I am going to retire in a year. Then my wife and I are getting an RV and we are going to live like nomads. I'm getting rid of possessions already. I would have sent him his hat back before, but I'm worried that mean son of a bitch would sue me. He would do it too."

"You're right. He would sue you. Tell you what. Send me the hat. I'll send it back to him. He already thinks I have it. Just send it to me."

"You'd do that?"

"Sure. I'll send him the hat. He won't do anything to either of us. Brent is terrified of me."

"Anybody sane would be terrified of you, Kato."

"Except you, Walt, right?"

Walt laughed. "Who said I'm sane?"

THREE WEEKS LATER

Brent Gardner was getting ready to help his ranch hands bring out hay for his herd of cattle when a FedEx truck pulled up to the Evictus Ranch main house. He signed for the package. Inside the box nestled in tissue paper was a hat. He recognized it immediately. It was his Roy Rogers cowboy hat, newly restored to perfect condition, cleaned and blocked.

Brent Gardner tried on his hat in front of a mirror. He moved it to the correct angle on his head. He smiled. The world felt just right.

PART 3
TROPOSPHERENCE

Leontes: "Go on, go on, thou canst speak too much of my black deeds. I have deserved all tongues to talk their bitterest of me."

Shakespeare, The Winter's Tale

Chapter 1

When Hoffman Bonaventure took the stage, the audience applauded. There had been no expectation about his appearance. He was short. He was oddly chubby with a slight barrel chest. His fringed bald head and dark eyebrows faded into the shadows created by the intense sparkle of his brown eyes.

He nodded as he approached the front of the stage. A slight waddle like a penguin accentuated his oddly shaped orthopedic shoes, the kind worn by dentists. He wore a short robe-like jacket that resonated with deep purples, blacks, blues, and greens. The tones changed when viewed from different angles. He was a walking shimmer, elegant and robust.

"You're all here because you **want** to be here. You're here because you **want** to transform. You crave a deep change in your life that you can't get anywhere else. Well you've come to the right place. You're now outside the box." Hoffman looked around the room and took his time shining his dark eyes into each person's soul. There were about twenty souls in attendance.

"Our method is complex and varied. We will be waking you up to your larger self, your higher self. In the same way a plant turns toward the sun, we will be turning you toward the celestial body that exists outside of you. Tropo, to turn, and sphere, meaning celestial body. We will be guiding you to a place outside of yourself that holds the true presence of the largest truth." Hoffman paused and glanced once again into each person's face.

"It is in some ways like slapping that old self awake, shaking that stuck-in-a-rut pattern that has kept you in your current slumber. You may feel slapped and profoundly jostled by the activities you will do here everyday. It is a full involvement of activity followed by self-reflection, sometimes followed by what we call 'happy family time'" Hoffman turned to walk left and turned again to walk back to his spot. During this motion, his head lifted to glance at the ceiling and he took a deep breath.

"You may feel disturbed by our program. That's good. You need to be disturbed. You may feel uncomfortable. That's the way it's supposed to feel if you want to get somewhere, to transform. That's why each of you will have a guide to meet with. These are gifted people dedicated to taking care of your personal work. They will at every step of the way remind you to 'mind your own process'. Everyone has their own process. Keep your attention on your own process. You have 40 days to break through, to hatch out of your own dead cocoon. This is your opportunity to be reborn as a special revolutionary animal. You will be propelled into a new life of constant transformation. Whether you are aware of it or not, there will be no turning back."

Hoffman took a sip of water and continued.

"This has been my calling for many years. You may not know my story. I only tell it to those who come here. Ten years ago, I was a podiatrist living in the suburbs of Mount Shasta, California. I was an avid hiker and loved being out in nature." His voice became emotional and quivered slightly as he told his story.

"It was in spring and I had just returned from a long hike. I had a glass of water and sat down at the kitchen table. My son Mike was reading in a chair against the wall. The next thing I knew was that I was in the room looking down at myself. The air was filled with a crystalline white glow. I felt ecstatic joy throughout my being. I was swooning, without thoughts or worries. I was love, there was nothing present but love."

He looked around the room again, smiling beatifically.

"You see, my friends, what I found out later was that I had collapsed and my son called an ambulance. I had died and was brought back to life nearly twenty minutes later. I had died and became Love. There is nothing but love here, whether you die or not. Since that day, all has changed for me. I am not the same person. I will never be that person again."

He took a sip of water and spoke again.

"What I want you to do during these 40 days is to die. Each of you in your own way needs to die and be reborn in order to get rid of the old baggage, the old dead weight you have been carrying around. You've been calling that old dead baggage, yourself. You're so much bigger than that. And we're going to slap you out of it, wake you up to where you are and who you really are. You are in space circling the stars, the spheres are out there talking to you and you cannot or will not hear them. And they are speaking in a language you do not know and cannot hear right now. This process is designed to make you turn toward the spheres and understand their unique message to you. After you leave here, you will have your own personal channel open to those spheres. You will hear them, and eagerly listen to the messages they have for each of you."

Hoffman Bonaventure gave his talk for the umpteenth time to a group of newbies. He was hopeful as always. His heart was open and his eccentricities were held at bay for the moment by the earnestness of his message.

"I know you are now wearing your training 'whites', you will find them to be your at-home outfit while you're here. They're loose fitting and you will automatically have them delivered fresh to your room every couple of days. Your other outfits are either in your closets or will be delivered to you. You'll be contacted by the tv monitor in your room and it will reveal the schedule for your day. Take a deep breath and relax. You're in a very safe space. As the days go by you'll understand how this retreat is helping you to nourish and thrive."

Hoffman's sibilant tone of voice had kindness and warmth in it. It was like a warm hand on the shoulder. The room remained largely quiet. A hand went up.

"Yes?"

"You look like Danny DeVito."

"And what is your name?"

"I'm Peter Marks."

"Thank you for sharing that. Are there any further questions?" No hands went up.

"Have a restful day. Thank you."

Hoffman turned his head and made eye contact with his stagehand and nodded. The man nodded back and left the stage immediately.

"Thank you all." Hoffman turned and left the stage.

The next day, Peter Marks was no longer attending the transformational retreat at Troposhperence International Healing Center.

Chapter 2

Early the next day, before the sun came up, Kato's TV screen came on and a kind sounding man's voice told him it was time to wake up and be ready in a half hour. The voice said "today will be your class in Rebabying. Wear the diaper, tee shirt and bathrobe that we put in your closet yesterday. No need to eat anything this morning. It's better if you have an empty stomach this morning. Food and drink will be provided."

Yawning with sleepiness, Kato showered, shaved and reached in his closet to find a diaper with flowers and teddy bears on it, and a tee shirt with bunnies, puppies and kittens playing together. The tee shirt had his first name stenciled on the back. The tee shirt was a little short, to show the world his belly. He dressed and looked at himself in the mirror and chuckled.

I look perfectly ridiculous.

It was just before dawn when he arrived at the big hall with the rest of his class. He was greeted immediately by a man and a woman who put their arms around him in a loving manner and led him inside.

"We are your parents today," the man said, hugging Kato. "Call me Daddy." He was about 20, with a concerned face. His 'Mommy' was equally nice and was probably in her 50's. The hall was dark, and soft music played. There were tiny igloo tents, barely big enough for a large child, set around the room, one for each member of the class. Mommy and Daddy directed him to his own igloo.

"Welcome," said a friendly man with a white beard, in his 60's. "My name is Marty Martini. I'm from Portland Oregon. I've been a professional Rebabying Instructor for 25 years. Your 'parents' have all been trained to act as your guides today. They are familiar with a few key facts about you. Trust them. Let them help you get the most out of today's experience."

"Rebabying started out as a workshop that took days to complete. However, we found we can successfully give a participant the full transformative birth to six years old experience in less than five hours."

He pointed at the igloo nearest him. "The first stage will be 'Prebabying.' You will be entering the womb, and when you emerge, you'll be able to experience a fresh start in life, emerging free of any trauma you hold inside you. When you hear the soft gong sound this morning, it means you've grown in age and are ready to enter another stage of childhood. Please note that the diapers can be used as diapers if this enhances your experience, however, your parents will show you that there are also urinals and bedpans."

Marty looked at the class.

"Let's get started. It's time to put on your Pre Babying birthing suit."

Kato's parents helped him step into a wrinkly, reddish colored one piece rubbery suit with a long umbilical cord coming out of the navel. They put light headphones on his head and directed him to enter the igloo.

"Curl up. Get comfortable. We will cover you with blankets. You are safe," said Mommy.

It was soft and comfortable inside. The umbilical cord was a little bothersome, but he arranged it and soon forgot it was there. The sound of a heartbeat along with soft gurgling abdominal sounds played in the headphones. Outside of the igloo he could faintly hear his parents singing to him as they rocked his igloo to simulate the mother moving through her pregnancy. The parents' song was just a few words, repeated endlessly: 'welcome baby Kato, we love you.'

Kato relaxed. He let the experience take him. It was goofy, affectionate, and harmless. He closed his eyes and drifted with the heartbeats and the singsong voices. He lost track of time, but it was not too long before the heartbeats increased, and the birth mother started experiencing discomfort, then extreme discomfort. Kato was alarmed. *So this is what I experienced before birth?*

The gong sounded. Suddenly, the igloo came off him, and he was in a darkened room with crying baby sounds in his headphones. Mommy and Daddy were near. They held him, kissed him and took off his birthing suit, singing 'Welcome Baby Kato, we love you.' They took away his earphones, swaddled him tightly in warm blankets, erected a large crib around him, and continued to sing, touch and celebrate baby Kato.

Kato relaxed and enjoyed the attention. The touching of his hands, feet and face felt genuine, the words were soothing.

Daddy said:

"I'm so sorry I left baby Kato. I'm here now. I'm not going to leave you." They gave him a bottle with warm milk. It tasted great.

Kato cried, and re-experienced the visceral childhood hurt, sadness, and anger that came when his father abandoned the family. He recalled the vivid ache he felt when his father ignored his letters and emails. He felt small and worthless. He was enraged. This pain intermixed with the sadness of his mother's passing. Mommy and Daddy held him tightly, kissed him and told him they would never leave. They lifted him up and put him in an adult sized baby stroller. They put a frilly baby bonnet on his head and placed a pacifier in his mouth.

"Goo goo goo," said his Mommy. She and Daddy then wheeled Kato around the room, meeting other parents and their 'infants', talking about them, gushing about how wonderful the babies were. The gong sounded. His parents wheeled him back to his crib.

Marty Martini's kind voice announced, "You are now almost one year old. You can leave your crib and crawl. You will be helped to take your first steps. You can only make sounds. Communicate with your parents, and be with them."

Kato crawled out. Mommy and Daddy encouraged him to crawl around all over them. They continued their supportive and affectionate talk.

On the other side of the hall, the Mommy and Daddy of another baby sang out, "Howie had an oopsie! Thank you. Oopsie doopsie, little Howie had an oopsie." Howie cooed and laughed along with the oopsie song. The parents busied themselves cleaning up Howie.

Kato stopped crying and cringed. *Ugh. You actually went there.* He saw the urinal nearby and decided that having a diaper accident was not going to be part of today's experience. *No thanks.*

After experiencing his first steps under the encouraging gaze of Mommy and Daddy with the rest of the class, the gong sounded and Marty Martini announced:

"You are now two years old. You can say a few words, and you are mobile. Go meet the other children if you wish."

The class wandered around blurting out baby words. They greeted each other with touch and sounds until the gong sounded and Marty announced:

"Three years old." They experienced more exploration and better articulation of language. Also, they were encouraged to go down a slide and use the swing set under their parents' guidance. Kato was having fun.

When the gong sounded again announcing 4 years old, he was moving away from the swing when a very attractive 20 something middle eastern looking woman with the name 'Preeya' stenciled on her shirt walked up to Kato. She had long, luxurious black hair. She put her arms around his neck and snuggled up close, purring seductively. Kato was startled by this advance and backed off. Preeya snarled and bit him on the arm, hard. She stood back with a triumphant expression to see if he would cry.

Kato moved away from her. He saw two men standing off in a corner. One was tall and skinny. His tee shirt said his name was Dylan. The other was shorter and barrel chested. His name was Jordan. They looked deep in conversation. When he got near them, they looked at him with warning frowns that unmistakably said 'get lost.' He gave them a thumbs up and backed off a few feet.

They continued their conversation. "I'm telling you, a credit default swap in this market is the best hedge against a cryptocurrency short sale position in Hong Kong," said the shorter man, "The numbers don't lie. Check your data."

Kato moved away. The image of two diaper clad men discussing international finance amused him.

Across the room Howie said in a high pitched falsetto voice "Howie has an oopsie! Oopsie doopsie whoopsie! Howie has an oopsie!"

Kato watched as the parents rushed to give him a second diaper change. Kato thought: *that's not a necessity, pal, that's some kind of fetish. He must love this stuff. Strange.*

The gong sounded for age five.

"Time for fun and games," said Marty.

"Make up a group game!"

Some ran, some sang, some wrestled, some held hands or put their arms around each other's shoulders and walked around. Kato lay on the ground playing a foot touching game with a group of five. Then they all rolled around together, and rolled each other around.

The gong sounded.

"You are six. Time for a brief nap. Gather near the swing set. Everyone get close together, hold hands." The parents brought mats and pillows. The class formed a close pile, and held hands. Kato realized this class was a good experience, even as goofy as it appeared.

When the gong sounded again, Marty said

"Congratulations. You have completed the Rebabying class." Kato's Mommy and Daddy came to him and held him in a warm, genuine embrace.

"Howie has an oopsie!" cried Howie in his fake high pitched childish voice. He sounded triumphant. "Howie has an oopsie doopsie poopsie!"

"Deal with it yourself," growled his exasperated Mommy, breaking her embrace with Howie and walking away.

Marty ignored this exchange. "What I would like for all of you to do now is go back to your rooms and write about your experiences in your journals. Write about anything that comes up. Savor and bask in this experience. The staff will bring your meals tonight. We will see you tomorrow morning here for a debriefing session about your experiences", instructed Marty.

Kato left. Back at his room, he started what would eventually become an ongoing letter to Irv. He wrote for hours.

The next morning at the small hall, Marty and the group had just taken their places for the debrief session, when Hoffman Bonaventure strutted in leading a group of Federal Marshals and FBI agents. Hoff pointed to Howie. The Marshals handcuffed Howie and the entire group left the room with Marty Martini.

"What the hell did he do?" said a large black man named Curtis, who looked like a former professional football player.

"Oopsie doopsie," said another person.

"Nah. Oopsie doopsie is definitely not a federal criminal offense," said another person.

"Probably not. It has got to be something else."

"How about crossing state lines for oopsie doopsie poopsie," said Curtis.

"No."

"How about crossing state lines with a minor for some of that whoopsie doopsie," said Curtis.

"Oh, yeah. That might do it. Sick puppy," said Jason.

Preeya, beautiful and mischievous looking in the baggy white judo outfit everyone was wearing, was slouching in her bean bag chair. She smiled, shook her head back and forth, and imitated Howie's whining and irritating sing-song voice. "Howieeeeee so baaaaad!"

When Marty Martini returned, Jason immediately asked the question on everyone's mind.

"What happened? What did he do? Spill."

Marty shook his head, "Never mind. It's not part of your experience. Mind your own process."

Chapter 3

A few days later, when Kato left his room in the morning he went directly to the Small Hall as his tv monitor directed. The blur of loose white outfits and joyful chatter passed him in the corridor. He walked slowly. He had been writing to Irv in his diary and his thoughts were still there.

He chose to write his thoughts to Irv, the person he had known the longest in life, because Irv was the last person alive who had witnessed him grow and develop and go through all the absurd issues and events that brought him to this very moment.

Today in his journal he confided in Irv about his anger and misgivings. He wrote about the loss of Phil. As Kato walked slowly to the class, his mind was still deeply in his journal. The inhabitants of the retreat flew past him and Kato walked in a slow meditative way savoring his thoughts and feelings. This is how his day began.

Upon entering the room, Kato sat in the formed circle on floor cushions beside his fellow retreat mates. The incense burned and the room was like a hushed church. The leader stood before them waiting for the moment of poised silence to begin.

"Today we will begin the arduous task of purging the past from our deepest parts. It is in these organic depths that we hold all our traumas. In our organs, in our cells, in our tissues. There it is kept until we call upon it to leave, instruct it to depart, let go of its hold on us. We can, each of us, remember and recall hurtful circumstances that repeat themselves, painful occurrences that have in some way guided our way or changed our paths. These traumas, whether we recognize or remember them, are still there. We may think they are gone, and we may have the sense that we have let them go and that now, because we are mature, grown up and on our own, are making sensible choices and decisions that don't regard any of these past foibles and traumas to bother us, to inform our discernment."

Kato listened intently. The woman who stood before him seemed like a professor. She spoke eloquently and deeply about the way the mind worked. He followed everything she was saying and applied it directly to what had happened to him with Phil, with Irv. His whole life was being dismantled. Although the folks around him were jostling around and seemed socially like school kids, Kato was taking it all in as if it were an IV.

"You think you are free from these traumas, and for the most part, you believe you are making a clear choice about what is required for you to do. I can tell you now that this is not the case. Our traumas must be consciously worked through. Once you are conscious of them, they will appear repeatedly so that you can choose not to allow them to cloud your judgment."

A young woman raised her hand.

"My dad punished me when I was a kid. I used to hide in the closet. Now everytime I feel bad, I want to go into the closet. But I stop myself from going into the closet. Is that what you're talking about?"

"I would say you are remembering the events from childhood and that you are resisting repeating the actions of childhood. However, the pain of what drove you to the closet initially is not being explored and expunged. Today we are going to get you to alleviate that moment. We have a support team that will guide you through the exercises. Each of you will have a person to work with. You will go to your own area in the room and work together. You will talk through the memories that are hiding inside. You will connect to the pain. And you will re-experience that same pain using the medicine we are passing to you now."

A man in white handed a small cup of fluid to each person as she spoke.

"Drink the medicine and think about that trauma."

"I don't have any traumas. I took a class just last month. I got rid of all my shit. It's gone. I don't really need to do this. So I'm going to exclude myself from this exercise."

"And what is your name?"

"I'm Carter." The man smiled proudly. He assumed he was way ahead of the class.

"Well you can be excused." The professor looked at her assistant and nodded. The assistant escorted Carter from the room. Kato never saw him again.

Kato took the medicine and drank it in one gulp. He immediately felt vulnerable. The woman who gave it to him helped him to stand and led him to a place in the corner of the room. He sat on a large pillow with her beside him. She began to converse with him.

"Kato, I believe you want the healing to be deep. I can see you are really working on some troubling things." She put her hand on his shoulder and for some reason he felt more vulnerable than he ever felt. Tears came to his eyes and he began to babble about uncle Phil and all the awful stuff he had done.

She patted him on the back and pulled out a plastic bucket. Without hesitation he vomited and began to cry at the same time. The deepest retching began and it took over his soul. It was as if he was in the throes of an emotional vortex that was scouring his being of all the shocks and traumas that had held sway over him.

He swooned and felt a nearly ecstatic eruption from his deepest gut level feelings. The loss of his father came up with its storm of tears and loss. His mother's death hurled forth in great sobs. His loving uncle Phil stood before him with tearing eyes and deathbed love and Kato cried uncontrollably. He had no inhibitions and cried inconsolably, easily, unendingly. His shameful behavior cascaded before him like a lewd cartoon, offensive and disgusting. He was heartsick over his awful actions.

She continued to pat his back and hold the bucket before him. When he finally finished crying and vomiting, Kato laid back onto the giant pillow. She wiped his mouth and patted his face with a warm towel. He felt comforted. She sat beside him and allowed her warm hand to sit on his shoulder. His shaky breath subsided slowly and he felt renewed, relieved. He had let it all out. There was nothing left to release. He was at peace.

"You did wonderfully, Kato. You made a fresh start." Kato took a long deep breath and let it out slowly.

"If you feel like sleeping, that's fine. I'll be right here beside you." She patted him again, softly. Kato thought she might be an angel, and fell asleep. He slept through the vomiting that took place around the room.

Some participants resisted vomiting and laughed in hysterical tones holding onto their composure, the composure that kept them troubled and untransformed. They would have other opportunities as the training went on, if they were willing to allow it to work.

In an hour, Kato woke up refreshed. His angelic support person walked him to his room and put him to bed. She gave him fresh water and told him to rest until he woke up naturally. When he woke up hours later, he was sure she was an angel. He was sure she was sent by some divine force to tend to him. He loved her.

Kato sat for hours writing in his journal.

Dear Irv, I'm so sorry, so ashamed for what I have done to you. You've loved me since I was a kid. We played ball together on uncle Phil's lawn. You gave me the childhood I always wanted. I didn't know that then. I know it now.

....

Down the hall, two suites away, one of Kato's training-mates, Albert Finestine, had a very different experience. After years of workshops and brief entanglements in his love life, Albert needed just another awakening to set his life on course again.

He had traveled over the world to find the gurus and shamans that would set him straight, correct his childhood of parental neglect and aimlessness. Albert had dabbled in everything he saw of value. Any cultural bauble that attracted his attention was immediately worthwhile. He was on the alert to be ahead of the curve and consequently tried everything that had come along.

From the hula hoop and the yo-yo to LSD and yoga, from communes and travels to the caves of India, Albert yearned to find whatever personal growth venue he could. Every workshop that promised a better life, miraculous achievements like holding his breath for an hour or staying submerged in Arctic temperature waters, Albert was on board. At least for the moment.

At each turn, Albert failed to find any sustenance in any of these deeply creative workshops and training seminars. Nevertheless, he was on board. His relentless spirit of exploration expected nourishment from each exercise he tried and this workshop would lead him through another exciting failure.

"You gotta just surrender to it bro." Albert said to a new found workshop buddy. Albert had just drunk the medicine and was walking and carrying his own pillow. He was accompanied by his vomit support guide, a formidable sized man with a kind demeanor.

"Yeah, Albert, yeah", his new friend responded, becoming deeply nauseous and consequently immobile. He sat on a pillow in the middle of the floor with his assistant, a willowy blonde woman who was struggling to support the man's folding and suddenly exhausted upper body.

As Albert passed he heard the groans of several of his classmates and cheered them on.

"Go with it folks. This is the path, this is the way. Let it go, release it. Get it out of your system." With this last word, Albert fell onto his knees on his pillow and began barfing hard. His support person held the pot before him and caught it all. Albert continued spasmodically until it was all out, at which time he collapsed onto his pillow.

"Now that was fabulous," his breath came hard, "What a great puke, ahh. I hope there's a little more, what a release, all that negative energy I've been holding onto. I can't believe after all this time there's still more." His breath came back and he shut his eyes, before he tried again to push out a bit more vomit.

"I know there's more in me. I'm not pure yet," he said smiling at his support person, his lips stained.

"It's okay, just relax for now." He patted Albert on the back. "Sleep if you can, it's good for you."

"Yeah but I know I can give more." Albert reached into his mouth with his pale fingers and forced them down his throat. He gagged a few times but nothing came up.

"I'm doing the best I can," Albert said, looking up at his support man, "I'm surrendering to the process, and now I'm empty and swooning, is that it?"

"Just relax Albert, it's okay, take a deep breath and relax."

"I know I need to do more," Albert said, his wet mouth pressed against the pillow.

"I've got to do more, this can't be all there is to it. I can vomit any time, there's got to be more." Albert fell into a deep sudden sleep. His open mouth breathing hard. His guardian watched him and said nothing.

Chapter 4

"The notion of the unconscious mind has been with us forever. Carl Jung spent years exploring aspects of this phenomenon and the influence of his exploration has extended deeply into the culture of personal growth."

It was several days after the creative vomiting class. Ms. Dodd, as she was called by the staff and students, stood quietly in her whites. Her kind and unblinking eyes were strange in their near colorlessness. Kato tried to determine if they were pale blue, gray or apricot.

Kato's morning had been taken up with a meeting with his personal guide. It was productive. Kato talked about his feelings of shame at having betrayed Phil and Irv. He spoke of the loss of his mother and was angry about his father's absence, an early trauma that he had mistakenly thought had been processed over the many years that had passed.

He was starting to understand that all traumas were in the mix, some were not actively at work and others were buried because the sensitivity to them had dissipated. Nothing triggered them any longer. Other traumas had become part of his mode of action and remained solidly in place, beyond any awareness of it.

"You may feel cautious in your approach to life. This attitude could be learned by enduring early traumas, old lessons that you are no longer aware of, but which, nevertheless, have become your way of being. These old pieces of lumber that clog the stream of your life are in your unconscious, weighing you down, slowing your awareness. As we go through this class, and the subsequent iterations of it that follow, you will be encouraged to observe the logs in your stream and determine whether you want them floating alongside your new deepened appreciation of who you want to be as your most significant and highest self."

Albert Finestine fidgeted on his pillow. He was trying to attain the lotus position so that he could perfectly cooperate with Ms. Dodd's narrative and be supremely open to any suggestions she might make. Receptivity, he learned, was a major part of embracing any new approach to attaining self knowledge.

"Albert, please relax, you needn't fuss," Ms. Dodd had been distracted by Finestine's constant eagerness and attempt to create boundaryless accommodations to her every word.

Per her suggestion, Albert took a deep meditative breath and consciously attempted to let go of all bodily tension. But he was trying too hard and his overt efforts distracted Ms. Dodd once again. She shook her head at him.

Unfortunately, Albert saw her chiding disapproval and it made him feel deeply insecure. He assumed that all his efforts had gone for naught and that he had displeased his teacher. He had failed, once again, to reach the threshold to the divine. His disappointment was obvious, and Ms. Dodd shook her head again before continuing her lecture.

"So let's begin our exercise with each of you making sure you are at a comfortable distance from our other participants. Slide your giant pillow over to a comfortable spot please. And I want you to lie back and sink into the ease and comfort of the pillow."

The class moved and laid back.

"Take a deep breath and relax. Let the energy flow through you. Rest deeply. This work is about letting it all go."

Ms. Dodd strolled among the pillows. She kept her eyes squinted gently to allow them to lose focus. It was her way of entering a gentle meditative state.

Finestine relaxed at last, only to realize that the fruit cup, and avocado toast he had for breakfast were doing combat in his gut. It was as if he was on a raft, and hands from the deep were reaching up to capsize his craft. He couldn't focus on what was being said. He felt gassy and knew the results would be unpleasant not only to himself but to his classmates as well. Despite his efforts to embrace and obey Ms. Dodd's directions, he stood quickly and left the room. Ms. Dodd was relieved that he was gone.

"Allow yourself to go quiet. Let your thinking slow and come to a stop. Thoughts will come and go, that's expected. Sink in, go deeper at every breath. Don't control anything. We are going toward the unconscious. We will rest on that blissful ridge, that borderland of eternity. This is where dreams come to meet you. Where dreams walk into your heart and instruct you. Here you will find your priorities, your advice from the divine. Watch and listen, let it unfold."

Her melodic voice rolled over and through Kato's mind. He was floating along, letting it all flow and pass through his mind. He was not in the hunt for anything. The images came and went as did his breath. All ease, no control. Kato was sleepy, nearly hypnotized. He heard the gentle snoring of the person nearest him.

"If you fall asleep, that's okay. It's fine. It's all fine. Be at ease. Allow this to happen. We are going toward becoming unconscious. And as we do, everything is acceptable. The more we do this, the easier it will be to become aware of the messages that are arising during this time. These messages are being given to us. They are gifts from the creative field of being. In these moments, we are being given divine direction. Just listen and relax. Let the voice be there; let the words be there. There is nothing you need to do."

Kato was fading into the reality of his own unconscious connection with his soul. He saw the image of Phil on his deathbed. He could feel the warm hand on the back of his head. He knew deeply at that moment that Phil loved him. The warmth of love spread over his body.

Dear Irv:

I didn't know how sad you were about your wife leaving and your divorce. You had a loss too. All I could think about was my loss. I've always been the baby whose dad refused him and whose mom died. I was so consumed with my own stuff I never knew how you felt when Lucille left.

I never considered how much you did for her, sending her to college and graduate school in Switzerland. And when you took me to see the Lakers so much. I know now it was because Lucille wasn't home, she was away. You must have been so lonely.

You shared your time with me. We had so much fun. Uncle Phil was mostly busy, but you were always there. I never understood your life, until now. Thank you Uncle Irv. I feel like you're my real uncle. Phil was great, but he was more like a king ruling over his domain. You were really the one who was there.

I think I want to get out of here, Uncle Irv. Maybe tomorrow will be the day I leave. I'm craving a line of coke. Every time I feel settled in and ready to be a happy man, I want to roll up a dollar and stick it in my nose. I'm angry at everyone around me, as if they're preventing me from having my cocaine and getting that rush. I blame them. I guess that's the first step. I know what I want and I'm not willing to get it. This sucks.

Chapter 5

The TV monitor alerted Kato that he would be attending another Happy Family Time social. He wondered what they would be doing this time. Each Happy Family Time Social was different. Some were silly. Some were instructive, but they all were friendly events with an emphasis on practicing good social skills. He put on the Family outfit that hung in the closet as directed. It was a festive and comfortable light off-white running suit.

He reluctantly made his way down the hall, still brooding about not being able to get a few lines of cocaine up his nose to numb out the sadness and the discontent that had been exposed during the emotions he was processing at Tropspherence. He snorted to himself like a barnyard animal.

When Kato entered the room the group was already assembled in a row each holding the shoulders of the person ahead of him. The speaker was playing the Bunny Hop. "Do the Bunny Hop, Do the Bunny Hop." The line of people hopped together at the words: "hop, hop, hop". It may have been a joyful way of expressing oneself at age eight, but now the repeated inane song was troubling.

The tune began to make him anxious. It brought back childhood memories of abandonment. How much more of this can I take, he thought. He kept trying to make it silly fun, but part of him was too raw and open to allow shallow fun. He replayed childhood parties. Insipid parents leaning over the group repeating sing song urgings for them to have fun. It wasn't fun, ever.

At best it was a time to put his arms around a pretty girl. To feel her body against his. Even at age eight, he felt the skin hunger that drove him to greater action and the semblance of intimacy. So lonely was he at that early age, so deep his abandonment and loss.

At that moment he felt hands on his shoulders. It was Preeya again. The dark skinned middle eastern woman. Her slender form and dark eyes clicked at him when he turned to look into her face. She smiled at him and moved her hands side to side. She was amused and energetic. He followed her lead and fell into a rhythmic Bunny Hop silliness.

For about a half hour, Kato forgot himself and was absorbed in the group. He thought about nothing, he analyzed nothing. He was present and allowed himself to be that way. He needed nothing and wanted nothing. For once in a great while, Kato exhibited joy, simple and uplifting. The relief affected his demeanor. His face took on a fixed smile that didn't leave during the entire party.

The leader took them on a journey of joy from one dance to the next. Group swaying, group hugging, group falling onto a giant pile of pillows. Kato was swooning with laughter and lightness. There was nothing heavy and burdensome. There was nothing to figure out or work through. He was merely present, and that was enough.

Music played throughout the Happy Family social. He danced by himself and with anyone and everyone who stood in front of him. The music went from silly childrens' music to rock and roll, to any other songs that conveyed joy and liveliness.

Preeya kept returning and putting herself in front of him. She was impossible to ignore, even if he had wanted to ignore her. He didn't. He was attracted to her intriguing eyes, and her soft hands that were always reaching out and touching him. She pushed him and prodded him, she turned him about, grabbed both his hands and led him in dance. She pulled him close, she pushed him away. All the while smiling into his face in the most charming and playful way.

Kato was indeed charmed. At one point she pulled him close and put her lips onto his neck. She sucked in the tender skin of his neck and moaned. She pressed against him tightly and danced him into an area away from the group. For a moment, Kato became more excited and he wanted her.

He returned her nuzzling and rubbed himself against her, as if they could fall to the floor right then and become deeply passionate. She put her mouth to his ear and whispered: "Later." She smiled into his face and danced them back to the group.

Kato was intoxicated by her. He watched her move about the room and join the group. She danced with everyone. Her caresses were not only for him, they were for anyone she fancied at the moment. She was moved to express her love.

Kato thought it was him only that she wanted. He remembered the bite she had given him during their Rebabying class. It had struck him then as a deeply childish act. Now he wondered if she was chasing him or the energy of life itself. He felt teased by her. Her capricious affection hurt when it was taken from him in favor of her own dance of life.

Before long, Kato was affirming his own joy once again in the throes of social connection. He danced and jumped around according to the beat of the music. The leader would occasionally shout a word out to evoke release.

"Let it go", she shouted, "Let the joy come through you, it belongs to us all. Share the release, express yourself, as you move freely. Yes, yes, that's it." She stood at the edge of the group and encouraged them to shine with love.

"You're bringing in the love. It's healing everyone you shine it on. Feel it glowing in your system. Radiate the love, the joy. It is a great benefit to feel this energy rushing through you. It quickens the soul." She was swaying and clapping her hands.

Those words resonated with Kato. "It quickens the soul." He wasn't sure what it meant, yet he felt it must be about the simplicity that allowed for his joy to rush out of him. That must be the quickening, he thought. That release of energy that passed through him, it wasn't his energy it belonged to everyone.

Preeya returned at the end of the class and took his hand. She looked at him with endearing eyes. She swung his arm with hers. They left together and she took him to the entry to his room. He opened his door and they went in together.

As soon as the door shut, she turned and pulled him to her. She held him tight and nuzzled her head into his chest.

For her part, she seemed to want to move and feel the depth of him coming and going from the deep warmth of her. But he realized this didn't feel right. For maybe the first time, he wanted more than a physical connection. He wanted the holding, the tenderness, the nourishment of his open heart. He didn't care about having sex. It didn't matter. He wanted closeness.

Kato was disappointed by her actions. He felt his heart was being ignored. Where had the sweetness gone?

She fought him and went back to grinding against him. Kato was disappointed and began to lose interest in the encounter. It was his first dry hump since high school. He felt ridiculous. Preeya sensed this. She looked down at him with disappointment and what he thought might be anger.

"I'm going then, sweet boy. Maybe some other time you'll appreciate me." She stood and left.

Kato lay on his bed. The joy and loving feeling that was hovering like a lush cloud in the room, became damp and uninviting. He curled into his blankets and held himself in the warmth. He thought that it might have been the first time he ever showed a woman his true wants. For the first time, he wasn't performing. He was coming from his authentic core; this was new for him. In this moment of what would normally be seen as being a failure to score sex, he was deeply satisfied with how he was embracing his truth, his real self.

What is happening to me? Six months ago, I would have been all over Preeya. This place is getting to me.

Kato fell asleep and was awakened by the TV monitor announcing that he would be meeting with his personal therapist in an hour. He had an hour to get ready.

Dear Irv: Last night was special. I don't know that I can explain it to you, but it was different from how I ever felt....

Chapter 6

Kato's personal counselor, Cora Willowbough, was 6'2". Her grace and ease was the result of years of tai chi and meditation and a full ride volleyball scholarship to UCLA. Her fame as a star forced her to process her priorities. Accordingly, she retreated and took care of her inner self and became a relentless practitioner in the human transformation movement.

Rather than towering over Kato, she sat immediately, and motioned to a plush chair. Her pleasant face was kind and unchallenging. She invited Kato with a smile. She was the "girl next door" he never met. He felt comfortable right away. He could tell her anything, sort through anything. It was magical.

"Why did you come to Tropospherence?"

"It was a combination of things." Kato began. He found himself talking about his loss of Phil and his mother's passing. He mentioned his father's absence in passing.

"Kato, this is just the beginning of our conversations together. I can see that you're carrying many traumas with you. Perhaps you're resilient too. Hopefully you've got a lot of strong good instincts, you're poised to break through." She poured a cup of tea for each of them and resumed.

"Try to let the Tropospherence experience work. There are so many who spend their time resisting. If that is how you treat this, your time will be wasted." Cora took a sip from the small cup that had been warming her hand. Kato took a sip too.

"It hasn't been easy, Ms. Will..."

"Call me Cora. Please. It's so much easier and we're getting to know each other. Have you made any friends here yet?"

"Well, I may have made an enemy last night. But somehow it felt good. Usually when I meet someone I'm attracted to, I start putting some moves on. This time, I didn't have that need to try, or perform, or invent who I was and appear a certain way to make myself appealing."

"How did you feel?" Cora asked.

"I was attracted to her. I just stayed with that feeling. And it turned out I wanted to get closer, more intimate. As we hung out a little longer, it became apparent that she wanted only sexual fun."

"And you didn't want that."

"It wasn't that I didn't want it. I was excited. I wanted that closeness I felt when we started hanging out. And as we got closer, the feeling changed.

She wanted an orgasm, I really wanted that intimate warm feeling. Don't get me wrong, she's a beautiful woman, I wanted her. It's just that I wanted the closeness more than the other stuff."

"You wanted close contact without the striving for orgasm or the performance that sometimes accompanies that situation." Cora stated.

Kato nodded, "Yeah that's right."

"Well I'm happy you stayed with your real feelings. If she's the real deal, she'll come back for the sweet and tender nourishment. You need not worry about how anyone responds to your choices regarding love and intimacy. There's a built in respect that is given when a person responds sincerely in a situation of intimacy. There is no winning or losing. I'm encouraged by your resolve to grow. And it's come so naturally, Kato. You're really on your way to a better, more profound life." Cora lifted her cup to him in a gesture of congratulations.

Kato felt like he might be emerging into the midst of a rich victorious life path. Her words fortified his spirit. He felt a warm glow that incited a deeply hopeful feeling.

"Let's continue later. If you have something specific you'd like to talk about, press 15 on the TV monitor and that will connect you to my cell phone, wherever I am. Otherwise, I'll let you know when we are ready to talk again. Remember, I monitor your progress throughout the program and I understand what you're going through. We'll talk about your childhood trauma next time you come in.

Cora stood and walked to him. Kato stood.

"Try to be a kind and gentle person, Kato. I'm very happy we met." She took his hand in hers and covered it with her other hand while she spoke, "You're making real progress, just be being here." She smiled warmly.

"Thank you, Cora." Kato lowered his eyes, turned and left her office.

Chapter 7

At 5 am in the morning Kato lay wide awake in bed feeling bored and generally irritated at everything. The feeling of connectedness he had with Cora yesterday was gone. Once again he wondered if this would be the day he walked away from Tropospherence. Increasingly, his inner musings were in that direction. The question was how to do it? *I could convince Preeya to leave with me, and we could fly to Puerto Vallarta on a lark. Of course we would get tired of each other in a couple of weeks, but it would be fun for a while.*

He had to admit to himself that he was becoming more secretive with each class. He had not shared his real inner thoughts or his escape plans with anyone, especially Cora. He hadn't talked about his longing for cocaine. He didn't trust anyone. Each class was designed to encourage honesty, sharing, openness and transformation, but he only went through the motions of authenticity. His only real opening up and honesty occurred during his journaling to Irv. When he was idle, in his room, he wondered if he could finish the Tropospherence course.

The past few days had been especially difficult for Kato at Tropospherence. With each phony interaction, where his only purpose was to fit in and fool others, he clearly witnessed himself disengaging, more and more. Yesterday was the second class in a series of classes about shame: what it is; how people unconsciously deal with it or hide from it; and tools for handling our shame in a positive way. Most of the class opened themselves up to the two skilful instructor therapists.

But not Kato. As soon as he sat down, he began inventing fake scenarios of things he had to be ashamed of, hiding all the real crappy stuff he had done. It seemed to work. When he was called on to share, he had a ready made fake story about him bullying a fictional schoolmate named Chadley. When pressed for details, Kato invented all sorts of future life troubles for Chadley. He expressed fake remorse for his part in ruining Chadley's life, and causing his suicide later on.

It seemed to have worked. Nobody questioned his story. Everyone felt his remorse for him. He hated them for it. His classmates seemed so fake. Everyone praised his difficult work towards personal growth. Someone suggested he write a letter to Chadley's parents. Kato said he would do it right away.

Kato turned on the bedside lamp, and reached for his IPad. He found the schedule for today's class. He groaned. Today's class was on power masks. No doubt Albert Finestine would find his power animal to be a lion, a magical gryphon, or some such nonsense.

While he lay there feeling bored, irritated and restless, he had a premonition: these feelings of irritation were familiar. They often preceded him getting into mischief, big trouble or causing pain or disruption in the lives of other people.

Screw it. Maybe getting kicked out works for me. Kato went back to sleep.

The power masks class started with a long lecture about the invisible masks that we wear to hide our true selves and our shame. Kato groaned inwardly. *More fucking shame.* The teacher was a woman in her 50's named Annabelle, who was an artist from Nevada. The rest of the class appeared very interested, even Preeya, and Kato decided on the spot that he would not invite her to escape Tropospherence with him.

In the second half of the class, Anna brought out art supplies of all kinds and invited each class member to create a mask that would represent their most powerful self. Kato just sat there, basking in his anger and disgust while the rest of the class started creating masks of all types. Finally, he went over to the art supplies, took a large pad of paper and a few colored magic markers and went to work.

His first couple of tries weren't right, but by the third try, he had his power mask. He cut out the eyes and held it up so everyone could see.

More than a few class members gasped when they saw Kato's creation. Kato's power mask was a grotesque and unflattering caricature of Hoffman Bonaventure, looking every bit like a sloppy, cartoonish Danny DeVito. He held it up and danced around with the mask in front of his face.

Chapter 8

Kato returned to his luxury cabin after mask class feeling angry at everyone. He was annoyed by everything at Tropospherence: the classes, the teachers, all of it. *What is the point? This is beyond stupid.*

Today he was particularly annoyed by Albert Finestine. The guy was so wishy-washy and weak. Kato had felt like unloading on Albert in front of the class but had controlled himself. Today Albert, as expected, made a power mask of a grizzly bear. He claimed he and his bear were on the verge of astrally projecting. A few days ago, it was Albert claiming a breakthrough in Yogic breathing. The day before, something else. Yada yada yada. *What a suggestable phony.*

He went to his fridge and pulled out one of the delicious nutritional shakes. He took a long swig. They were good, he admitted to himself.

The doorbell rang. The flat screen TV immediately showed who was ringing. It was Cora Willoughby. They didn't have an appointment.

"Hi Cora. I didn't realize we had an appointment."

"We don't. I heard about your class today, and decided to come by to see you."

"Oh. Okay."

She entered. After declining his offer of a shake or other refreshment, she set her handbag down on the floor and looked at him.

"Kato, are you alright? Annabelle, the mask making class instructor noticed you today. She called me. She said you looked moody. She said you looked angry and distracted. She said she caught you 'sneering at the other class members.' Her words – not mine."

"Was it that obvious?"

"Apparently. Ok. What's wrong? What are you holding back? How about if you just tell me. Don't waste our time please. No bullshit."

Cora's blunt manner stopped him from blurting one of his usual glib, defensive, deflecting responses. She sat back on the sofa. She was examining him closely, but not unkindly.

He took a deep breath. He let it out slowly. He realized this was a turning point. If he wasn't honest here, their therapeutic relationship was probably over, or not worth continuing.

"Ok. You want to know?"

"Yes. That's what I'm here for."

"I don't know why, but I'm angry. I'm angry all the time. I'm angry at the participants. I'm angry at the instructors. I'm angry at fucking Danny DeVito Hoffman. I seem to work myself into a fury at anyone who is really participating at Tropospherence in any way. I think this place is phony. I'm furious at you Cora. I like you. You seem genuine. But you're participating in this complete nonsense."

Kato was breathing heavily. He stared at Cora defiantly.

"Can I offer an observation, Kato?"

He shrugged. "Go ahead."

"I may be wrong, but sometimes when someone finds themselves in a perpetually angry state, it can mean that they are close to uncovering some uncomfortable truth about themselves, something they would rather not face. All of us will do anything to hide from shame."

"You think that's what's going on with me?"

She smiled.

"*Do you* think that's what's going on with *you?* It doesn't matter what I think."

Kato snorted. They looked at each other for a long minute. Neither spoke. Kato thought about his obsessive anger. He grudgingly admitted to himself that she might have a point. Why was he so angry all the time at such little stupid things?

He let out a sigh.

"I wish I knew why I was angry. It seems stupid of me."

"It's not stupid. How do you feel about your anger today?"

"Today? Trapped. It just keeps coming up."

"I get it. You're trapped," she said.

"This place is getting to me."

"Can I make another observation? Again, I might be full of shit."

"Yes. But I have a question of my own."

"What is it?"

"Did you drive all the way from Santa Barbara to see me today?"

"Yes. I came here to see you. Hoff called me. Annabelle thought you were about to act out inappropriately. Before you did, Hoff wanted to give you one last chance to see if together we couldn't pull you back from the brink."

"It almost sounds like you care."

"I'm trying to care. I want to believe in you. I'd like to like you," Cora paused and took a deep breath, "Let's get one thing straight. I'm not going to blow smoke up your ass and tell you you're a wonderful person making great strides in your life. Before I came here, I read your file. I read that tabloid news story, *Cain Enabled*. I can't ignore it. You've been creating victims for years," Cora said angrily. "I'm not afraid of you Kato. You're here, maybe you're actually trying. That has to mean something, right? Because it feels like you're making an effort, I'm interested in you. I ask myself: Can he be helped? And I also ask myself: Should I help him? I don't like wasting my time, and habitual predators like you can kiss my ass."

Kato was shocked. The formerly kind, understanding and supportive Cora was shoving his life of bad deeds down his throat. It hurt.

"You said you had another observation. What is it?" Kato asked, bracing for the worst.

"When I was thinking of you before I got in my car, I thought: what if Kato is trapped? What if Kato is a slave to his impulses? Seemingly out of nowhere, one of my heroes, one of the greatest Americans of all time, Frederick Douglass came into my mind. I wondered if his life story could help put your life into perspective. Have you ever read his autobiography?"

"No. I know his name, but that's all."

She reached into her handbag, and handed him a slim book.

"Kato, I think you could be a slave to your impulses, your obsessions, your patterned responses, your repeated bad behavior, and your self-justification. I believe you might be a slave to your rage."

"A slave. Isn't that a little harsh?"

"Maybe. You decide. Read the book. And if you find yourself tossed out of this place, then it's my parting gift."

Kato read the title aloud. "Narrative of the Life of Frederick Douglass, 1845 Edition. Are you firing me as a patient?"

"Maybe. That'll be up to you. This place, Tropospherence, is all about transformation. It's for real. You might be treating it like a joke, it's not. If you continue to sit here and stew over your petty grievances and irritations without looking at the big picture, and you make no effort to change, why should I waste my time with you?"

Kato looked at the book cover with its picture of a distinguished African-American.

Cora saw Kato's interest.

"He published this book when he was 27. He was a nobody. He was a slave on the run. After publishing his book, almost overnight, he became one of the most famous Americans of the 19th Century. He was known all over the world. He was the most photographed American of his era, even more than Abraham Lincoln."

Cora continued excitedly. "His story is remarkable. While he was a slave, he was whipped regularly. This went on until he was 20, when he risked everything to escape. He knew that if he were caught, he would be broken and sold into the slave markets of the deep south. He knew he'd never get out."

"What does that have to do with me?" asked Kato.

"Just listen. You've been pampered all your life, but Douglass went through the full range of atrocities of slavery, and overcame more than we could ever imagine. For example, imagine this: when he was nine, his old master died and the heirs traded him along with a few pigs and cattle. His new master lived in Baltimore. But all of Douglass' brothers and sisters and cousins were lost forever in the cotton and cane fields of the deep south. Can you imagine that? Douglass' new master's wife gave him a couple of reading lessons, but when her husband found out, he was furious and he stopped the lessons. But the flame for learning was kindled, and Douglass began his relentless, lifelong craving for intelligence. He taught himself secretly to read, and then coaxed some immigrant street kids to teach him to write. He spent his life trying to make sense of his enslavement, and of humanity."

"Douglass was trapped in a corrupt, inhumane system. He used his courage, intelligence, and imagination to bring attention to human enslavement. He absolutely made the world a better place. He fought for equal rights for women too, long before any other man. He never stopped."

"Look at what he overcame and achieved despite all the hardships and torture he had to endure. Kato, think about what Douglass went through, and then look at yourself!"

Cora's voice rose as she pointed at Kato.

"Look at yourself. Here you are with unlimited privileges and resources, nursing your petty resentments, and annoyances. Waa Waa Waa. Are You making the world a better place? No!" Cora continued loudly, "If you don't think it's time for a life change I can't help you! I don't want to waste my time on you. Where's your courage? And don't bullshit me. Either you do the difficult work or you go back to your depraved life of excess and predation. What do you wanna do? Your choice."

Her loud voice filled the room. Then she got up and left. Kato was stunned.

He sat for a moment, then proceeded to read the entire Frederick Douglass book in one sitting. He finished at 10pm. He was captivated by the inspiring story of resilience and courage. Compared to Douglass' ordeals, Kato felt small, mean, worthless, and defective.

Cora was right, he thought. I'm a slave. But not just a slave. I'm also the slave owner, and I'm the overseer with the whip in my own hand. I'm trapped in my compulsions.

Kato felt deep aching despair. He pondered how he could have created this cage for himself? Douglass could blame the system, but there was no one Kato could blame except himself. There was nobody who could fix this but himself. All his pointless, petty anger from earlier in the day vanished. It was replaced by a fervent desire to change. He was terrified he would fail. He decided he would try to do whatever it took. Douglass' life inspired him, and with that inspiration he stepped out for a walk into the summer night.

There was a full moon. He took a path into the hills. As he neared the top of a steep hill he heard the sound of moaning. He looked around. The sound came from off the trail.

"Hello?" He called.

"Help me," answered a woman's voice, very faint. "I'm coming. Keep talking. I don't have a flashlight."

Kato scrambled down the rocky hillside until he came to the woman. It was Kathy, a 50-ish participant at Tropospherence. She was clutching her shoulder and grimacing. She was wearing shorts and flip flop sandals.

Kato knelt down. "I'm here. It's me, Kato. I found you. The worst is over. Tell me where it hurts."

She didn't answer. It was like she was miles away. She shivered, even though it was warm. Kato took off his shirt and covered her.

"Kathy. It's going to be alright. I see your shoulder hurts. Your other shoulder looks ok. Is that right?"

She nodded.

"Good. I see you're holding your shoulder. Can I hold this hand?" She nodded. He held the hand of her undamaged shoulder.

"This hand is strong. That's good. Can you tell me if you are hurt anywhere else?"

"Head hurts."

"Ok. I see that you hit your head. But I see that you're moving it. That's good. Look at me." Kato smiled at her. He lightly touched her head. There wasn't much blood.

"It's not bleeding. That's really good Kathy. Is there pain in your legs? Can I touch your feet to see if you can move your toes?"

She nodded.

"You can move your toes, Kathy! That's very good. I don't have a cell phone. Is it ok if I leave you for a bit and go get help? Will you be alright?"

She nodded. "I'll be right back Kathy. I promise."

He ran back. Then, followed by staff, he ran back to Kathy. He stayed with her over the next hour, holding her hand and speaking softly and encouragingly, while the paramedics transported her back down the trail and off to the hospital.

Kato stayed with Kathy all night in the hospital until the next day, when her family arrived. The doctor diagnosed shock, a concussion and a dislocated shoulder. She was expected to recover. She said she intended to return to Tropospherence. After Kato got back to his cottage, Hoff knocked on his door.

"That was good work last night, Kato. I want to thank you. You kept your cool. I just talked to Kathy. She says you were a real comfort. Do you have EMT training?"

"No. I didn't even think. I just did what I thought needed to be done."

"I think you might have a knack for it. One thing I know about rescue work is you will never get bored. Do you want to skip class this morning?"

"No. Whatever it is, I want to be there."

"Good man."

Chapter 9

The next day, Kato's newfound enthusiasm for personal growth at Tropospherence evaporated the very second he walked into the large hall for the Anger and Grief class and saw that the teacher was Hoffman Bonaventure himself, standing puffed up and proud, wearing a salesman's smile and a tan three piece suit that seemed to accentuate his chubby belly.

Kato groaned. Suddenly, all of his usual irritation at Tropospherence flooded back, along with all of his fatigue from staying up last night helping Kathy at the hospital. It felt like the right day to walk away. He folded his arms defensively, slouched in his bean bag chair and yawned.

"Welcome," said Hoff. "Everyone, push the chairs off to the side. Pick a partner. Spread out. Find a place on the floor."

Kato didn't move. Soon, everyone had a partner. He was the odd man in the class, still sitting sullenly in the bean bag chair.

Hoff saw this, smiled and said: "I'll be your partner Kato. Come over here."

Kato knew this was his best moment to walk away from Tropospherence forever. He almost did it, but for some reason he held back. Maybe it was inertia or fatigue, but whatever the reason, he kicked the bean bag roughly over to the side of the room, and petulantly strolled over to Hoff. He was at least a foot taller than the diminutive fat man, and he purposefully looked down at Hoff, who smiled sweetly up at Kato, making him angrier.

"Let's get right to it, class. We are going into some very dark territory today. I want you to give it everything you have."

Kato slouched and stared off at a far wall.

"I want you to stand about four feet away from your partner. Look him or her in the face." The class moved into position.

"Good. Now take a minute to decide who is that one person in your life that you are angriest at. Who is most deserving of your anger? Don't talk about it. Don't name the person. Just decide who that person is in your life. Who are you most angry at?"

The class stood there for a couple of minutes. Each person was lost in his or her thoughts. Kato heard Hoff, but shuffled his feet around like a moody child.

"Ok. Have you decided?" Everyone nodded.

"Great, now I want you to take turns screaming for two minutes all of your anger in the face of the person opposite you. You are screaming at the person who hurt you the most in your life. Scream your heart out at the person who hurt you the most. Your partner is innocent. They are hearing you. They are witnessing you. No touching. No contact. Stay four feet apart. Keep your hands behind your back. But otherwise, go completely insanely crazy with anger. Scream till you are hoarse and red in the face. The person who isn't screaming just stands there and accepts all of that anger, hears it, but doesn't comment or react. Don't react in any way!"

Hoff took a deep breath.

"Kato, you wait. You'll get your turn in a while. Ok class, decide who's going first."

The pairs looked at each other and decided.

"Ready, set, go!" The class erupted in howling screams. It was raw. It was real. Kato was impressed.

At the end of two minutes, which seemed to go on forever, Hoff stopped everyone by waving his arms. The panting screamers all were breathing heavily.

"Switch around. The screamer last time is now the listener. Are you ready? Set? Go!"

A second round of howling filled the hall. When it was over, Hoff called time.

"Catch your breath everyone."

Then he turned to Kato.

"Stand about four feet away from me."

"I think this is bullshit, *Hoff*," sneered Kato, emphasizing Hoff.

"So it's bullshit? You mean, you don't have anybody who hurt you the most in life? Everyone has been wonderful to you?"

"No. Of course I've been hurt. But I have a problem with you, your whole phony program here. It doesn't do any good. Not for me at least. It's useless."

Hoff nodded.

"Let's try something different, Kato. First of all, tell us the name of the person who hurt you the most. Who are you angriest at? Who is it?"

Kato shrugged. "Not that it is going to help, but I know who that person is."

"Who?"

"It's my father. Ok?" Kato thrust his chin at Hoff. "Are you happy that I said it?"

"Ok. It's your father. Is your father still alive? Do you have any contact with him?"

"No. He's a piece of shit. He's German. He abandoned my Mother. I tried to contact him several times when I was ten, after my Mom died. My Father never answered my letters or my emails, not-even-once. He even changed his email address deliberately to avoid me."

"That is bad. That really must have hurt."

Kato didn't answer. He was getting angry, his fists balled up at his sides. He didn't like being exposed when sharing about his Father.

Hoff nodded. Softly he said "Let's try something now, just you and me, Kato. I'll be your father. Pretend that I am. Go ahead and ask me anything that you would want to ask your Father. I'll answer for him. What would you say to your father? what would you ask him, if he were standing right in front of you right now? Do it."

Kato took a series of shallow breaths. He was starting to lose self control. His eyes bored into Hoff, who was easily in punching distance.

Then he whispered: "Why?"

Hoff indicated with his eyes for Kato to keep going.

"Why did you leave us? Why didn't you answer my letters? I was just a little kid. Why? Why?"

Hoff nodded. He waited a bit, then said quietly:

"Kato, my son, I didn't answer you because it hurt me too much. It just hurt too much."

"What? It hurt *you*?" Kato's voice dripped with scorn.

"Yes. It hurt me. I just couldn't stay. I couldn't face you. I couldn't face your mother while she was alive and she was the only one caring for you. I just couldn't be there. It hurt me too much. Thinking of you made me feel worthless and defective, I felt like a piece of shit father."

Kato's face was deep red. He was breathing heavily.

"Kato. As your father, standing in front of you, I want you to scream at me. I want you to let it all out. All of it. Ready? Set? Go!"

Kato screamed like he was suffering all the torments of hell in one moment. He sputtered, spat and cursed his father. Then he just screamed without words. On and on he went. It went on a lot longer than two minutes. Finally he just stopped. He was panting.

Hoff stood in front. Calmly he said: "Kato, my son, I hurt you so much. You were just an innocent child. You didn't deserve it. I'm worthless. It hurt me too much to see myself as the failure I was. I was so selfish. Kato, I am so so sorry for what I did to you. I am so, so sorry. I really mean it."

Kato broke down and fell into Hoff's arms. He bawled and bawled. Hoff started crying with Kato, no doubt reliving his own inner trauma. The entire class came around and surrounded Kato and Hoff, all of them tightly hugging each other in the center. Spontaneously, they all started crying about their own wounds. Together they were a wailing, crying, moaning, swaying and grieving mass of bodies. It was wordless. It was primeval grief, the same group grieving as what was once shared by ancient tribes all the way back to when humans lived in caves. They moaned and cried, and swayed together in one tight group of crying bodies.

Finally, fifteen minutes later, they ran out of tears. They simply held each other in their tight, swaying group and they hummed, low and sad to one another. Kato felt exhausted, spent, and safe. His heart opened. He loved them all. This went on for several minutes.

Then, unseen by anybody, a staff member turned on music and the unmistakable sound of Zorba the Greek's dance of joy started playing, filling the hall. Huddled together, they heard 20 balalaikas start playing slowly. The group started moving slowly, still huddled together. Then the song sped up, and the group formed a big circle and they all danced.

Going faster and faster with arms around each other's shoulders, kicking out, and changing directions. They danced ecstatically, laughing and smiling.

Joy flooded in Kato. He felt love towards everyone. He kissed each person next to him on the cheek. Then the song ended, immediately followed by another recognizable song, Hava Nagila. The group immediately improvised and danced and clapped and the room was filled with love.

Other songs followed, a corny square dance type number, then Dancing Queen by ABBA. They danced and danced for over an hour. It was the most fun that Kato could remember ever having. All of his earlier irritation was now gone. His fatigue was gone. Finally, when everyone was spent and sweating, the gong sounded.

Hoff shouted: "Let's feast!"

They walked to the next room where one long banquet table was set for all of them, filled with sumptuous food and drink. They sat, still embracing each other like long lost soulmates, and ate and drank till they had their fill.

Sitting among them, and one of them in every way, Hoff smiled to himself. He thought: *Now this group has come together. It came a little bit later than usual, but everyone finally made it. Kato made it too. We are all one now. Now the real healing work can begin.*

Chapter 10

Six months later.

The small box was at the door when Irv went looking for the morning paper. The sunlight hit his eyes as he leaned to grab the plastic wrapped LA Times.

He modestly held his robe closed as he bent to pick it up. He shook the box as if it would tell him all it could reveal. He opened it. It was Kato's journal. It was unexpected. This was his first contact with Kato since Phil's death.

He took it back inside his now refurbished mansion, sat in his favorite chair, and immediately started reading. The journal simply began with the words 'Dear Irv'. That got his attention. He learned about the intimate revelations about life during Kato's transformational time at Tropspherence.

Irv spent his morning reading the journal like a starved man eating a bowl of grits. He looked up from the table, his unfinished coffee, cold and neglected, his eyes blurred by tears.

....

It was Sunday at Kato's modest house in a beachfront suburb north of Santa Barbara. As usual, every day, Kato meditated upon waking at 5 am, then he ran five kilometers along the beach. Afterwards did his tai chi form and worked through his chi kung set.

Sunday was his only day off. He looked at his busy schedule for the coming week. Tomorrow he had another helicopter pilot lesson. Soon he would fly solo. Flying was such a rush. He loved it more than he had once had loved drugs. He also was in his tenth week of EMT training at the community college. This coming week he had ambulance training rides scheduled. The newness of each emergency call, the need for quick action, the lives saved, or not saved, it all excited him. He knew he would obtain his goal this year to become first an EMT first responder, then later, a helicopter EMT pilot. He had it all planned out, and he couldn't wait.

Kato looked out over the beautiful hillsides that lead up from the beach at his new place. He thought about how lucky he was to be living here, far from his former life of Los Angeles decadence. One of his big realizations from Tropospherence was that he had an addictive and self destructive personality. He now knew that drugs and alcohol and power grabbing and game playing would only lead to a general relapse. Knowing this, he had sold his L.A. apartment before graduating from Tropospherence. He still had his millions from GRAB Training, so he bought this house to be near his personal counseling sessions with Cora Willoughby, and to her weekly therapeutic group sessions. It pleased him to be in a place where nobody knew him or cared who he once was. Reinventing himself was thrilling.

After looking at his schedule, he began some Pilates work. The phone rang.

"Hello, Kato speaking."

"Kato, it's Irv. I just read your journal. It touched me. It's amazing. I want to come see you. Are you going to be around today? I can be there in about an hour or so."

"Irv, please come by. I'd love to see you."

"I'm on my way."

While Irv dressed and got into his car, Kato called Cora.

"Cora, Irv is coming by today. I'm excited, but I'm also a little worried. He's a huge figure from my past, and a big reminder of my failures." Kato had developed a positive counseling relationship with her. He treasured her.

"Kato, that's great. What a wonderful opportunity for you. We can talk later today if you need it after meeting with him. Otherwise, just savor your time with him."

"I will. Thank you, Cora."

"Of course. Talk later."

Kato breathed in the ocean air. He opened the windows and doors to let it fill his house along with the sound of the waves. Excitedly, Kato tidied his house and put on a pot of soup. He knew that Irv loved soup.

In what seemed like minutes, Irv arrived at the door.

"Irv, so good to see you."

"Kato, I can't believe this. I read the journal. You started each entry with 'Dear Irv'. It touched me. I just don't know what to say. I'm overwhelmed. I had to see you." Irv stepped forward through the doorway and took Kato in his arms and pulled him tightly to his chest.

"Why didn't I see this?" Irv kept repeating, his eyes filled with tears, "You pushed me away for so long that I thought you were gone from me forever. Oh my god..." Irv pulled his head away from Kato's shoulder for a moment and looked up at him.

"You're like the son I never had, before you pulled away. And all this time, I thought you hated me. But that wasn't it. It was your trauma. Oh my dear boy. How could I have known? I'm so sorry this happened to you, but

I'm so happy you're here now. Thank you, thank you." Irv cried and hugged Kato.

"Irv. I want to tell you that I realize now that you were the glue in my life. You held me together throughout all the crazy stuff I went through. All the empty chasing after pleasure, the self abuse. Phil let me get away with doing it, but I needed boundaries, and you were the strong one. I disrespected you and I'm ashamed of that, but you were there for me, by not buying my bullshit. I went way off the deep end, but it was you who tried to stabilize my life. I loved Phil, but he was taking care of me because of my mom. Not you, Irv. I now realize that you loved me, you always loved me. From the very beginning." Kato held Irv and tears rolled down his cheek.

Kato knew he had found a true father figure. They stood holding each other until Kato smelled the soup boiling away.

An idea occurred to Kato, something that had been rattling around in his mind, something that he needed to do as part of his recovery and restitution to the world. Up until now, it was unobtainable, because it was something he could not do all by himself.

"Irv, I have an unusual project that I need help with. You would be the right person to help me. I can't do it myself, because it requires getting involved with people down in L.A. in the show business world. That scene is permanently toxic for me. It's unhealthy. If I went there, I could relapse. I'll pay for everything to make this happen. However, my involvement must be anonymous. Only you can know that this idea comes from me. OK?"

"I'll do whatever I can to help you avoid relapsing, Kato. Not after you've come this far. Tell me about your idea. If I can help. I'll do it."

Kato told Irv about the project. Irv agreed to help, and he agreed that Kato's involvement would remain secret.

They spent the next couple of hours telling each other stories and remembering. They took a long walk on the beach and imagined a future that would involve spending some more time together. As they were saying goodbye, Irv paused. He was smiling.

"Congratulations, Kato. I don't know how you did it, but you found your way back to becoming that sweet, kind and generous person you once were as a child. We never stopped hoping. Now here you are. You did it. It is remarkable. I am proud of you."

Chapter 11

As usual, Alec Finch was in his apartment watching game shows at 2pm in the afternoon. He was wearing his rumpled plaid bathrobe, which is what he wore all day long. Since the collapse of Socio-Ortho Genomics, he rarely left his apartment, except to buy food and go out to play music from the 80's with his garage band. His only other regular contacts were with his Mother, and with his old friends from the Rock Star Hair Club. He had money saved, but he was not a happy man.

His phone rang, while he was staring at Vanna White in a stunning slinky dress while trying to solve the Wheel of Fortune puzzle.

"Alec Finch?"

"Yeah. That's me. Who are you?"

"My name is Orin Wheeler. I am with the Norris Fletcher Talent Agency. We book musical groups to tour and play at Native American casinos all over the west and midwest. I'm putting together a 1980's style touring band. We are calling it 'The Rod Stewart Tribute.' We need a bass player. I have seen some footage of your bass playing and your backup singing. You would be on the road for six months. If it goes over well, the band will get more gigs all around the country. There will be a tour bus, roadies to set up the shows, and the works. You will be treated like stars. Would you be interested in trying out as our bass player?"

Finch was so stunned he couldn't answer.

"Mr. Finch, are you still on the line?"

Earlier that day, Orin Wheeler had reassured Irv Gottlieb again that he would never tell Alec Finch that Kato Worsen was the man setting up and financing this tour.

"Mr. Finch, are you still with me?"

"Yes," Finch whispered.

"Are you interested? We think you would be a good addition to the band."

"I don't know what to say."

"Say yes."

"It would be my dream job, so yes, yes, yes, I am interested."

"Excellent. I do have one question: The band members must wear 1980's rock star hair cuts. Do you still wear your hair styled in a 1980's fashion? From what I see from your old band photos, your haircut would look good for this band.

"Yes."

"Excellent. I will send you an agency contract, and tell you where the band will meet to practice. I hope you can clear your schedule right away. This is happening very soon."

When the phone call ended, Finch couldn't believe his luck. One phone call had just turned his life around completely. He immediately picked up his phone and called his Mother in Bristol, England. He was jubilant.

"Mum. I have fantastic news. I'm going on the road with a professional band, playing my favorite music. Even better, the tour will be called 'The Rod Stewart Review'! Can you believe that? The tour will have a bus, crowds, great pay, everything. This is what I have always wanted. I've made it!" he said giddily.

"That's so nice son. I have always believed in you."

THE END